Ally Cat

A Tale of Survival

Enjoy! ♡
Kathy J Shields

By

Kathleen J. Shields

This book is a work of fiction. Places, events, and situations in this story are purely fictional. Any resemblance to actual persons, living or dead, is coincidental.

ISBN-13: 978-1-941345-11-5 Paperback
ISBN eBook: 9781301950072 (Smashwords)
ISBN-13: 978-1-941345-22-1 CreateSpace

Canyon Lake, TX
www.ErinGoBraghPublishing.com

Chapter 1

It was a cold, dark and rainy night when it happened, the same as tonight she thought to herself. The city was blacked out preparing for night raids, but she just walked down the street without a thought about that oh-so-distant situation. She probably should have been concerned, she probably should have searched for cover but as she continued down the street, basically tuning out the sirens, she focused her attention on her own personal situation instead. How on earth had she got herself into such a predicament, was beyond her imagination. It had been a couple of weeks now and still, every time her eyes opened from her slumber she wondered if *this* was the dream. Certain that her dreams were the real life and this, this was the nightmare, she'd then stretch, rise to her feet and begin her ascent into this amazingly realistic unknown.

This night, however, she was preoccupied with something bigger than her curiosity of this dream. This night would have to be about the hunt for food, which was fast becoming a necessity. Starvation was beginning to set in, and she knew she wouldn’t have the strength to go much further if she didn’t find something to eat soon. As her stomach grumbled and she heard the sounds of its upset so vividly, she still couldn't believe it was her own stomach. Everything was foreign to her. As she padded down the sidewalk, she spotted her reflection in a darkened store window and stopped to look at herself. She looked pathetic. Her eyes were tired, her face drooped down, her hair was all matted; she was ashamed of herself. But most of her shame was contributed to her new look; a scary face looked back at her in the reflection and it made her shiver. This face was harder for her to accept than anything else in her life right now. When she looked at herself, her body, she wanted to vomit. When she looked at her face she wanted to claw her eyes out. When she looked at her face, she saw that of a feline and that was definitely not what she was supposed to see.

You see, she wasn't always a cat. Just a few short weeks ago she had a name, Miss Goldie, and she had a career as a scientist's lab assistant. She was a human woman who had lived a human life of science. Long flowing hair, gorgeous green eyes, as skinny as a rail, she thought to herself, that was me then, and oddly, that is me now. Her long gold fur was dirty and knotted, her green eyes looked so tired and her skinny stature just accentuated her hunger. Her once soft paws were now cracked and blistered and they hurt as she walked on the rough cement.

She had been through quite a bit the past two weeks. The sheer knowledge of what being a cat was like in this world was enough to make her want to do everything she could to save them; if she were still human. That was the hardest thing to deal with, the people. She never considered herself a bad human but after being a cat for a few days she learned that most cats would consider humans to be bad news, whether they intended to be or not. People in a hurry to work would walk right by her, not even notice her, some would run right into her, kicking her or stepping on her tail, others would just ignore her. She spent the first three days of her life as a cat trying to communicate with the humans. Trying to tell them her story, trying to get someone to help her, of course they didn't understand her cries and meows. She spent the next three days trying to get their attention through stealing their food, that didn't go over well. She spent the days after simply trying to figure out how to survive without human assistance, she was failing miserably.

After making her way back to her home, miles from the city where she worked, she finally came across her boyfriend. She assumed by his looks that he was distraught that she was missing. He looked tired, like he had been up for hours and almost sick, like the grief was making him ill. She felt so bad for him, wanting to comfort him to tell him she was all right and that she was here. She went to the door and pawed at it. Yowling at the top of her lungs to get his attention. But all she got was a yell back. "Go away, you filthy cat!" At first she was startled. He had always embraced her passion for cats; he said he liked cats but his attitude now showed differently. But she continued nevertheless, assuming he was too upset to pity a stray cat.

Goldie knew in her heart that when he saw her, that when he looked into her eyes he would see her, he would somehow know it was her no matter how ridiculous it sounded and he would do something to help her. But when he did come out and finally saw her he showed no caring or compassion, in fact what he did show her was the tip of his boot as he kicked her from the front stoop. Ten feet away now and catching her breath she stood back up and looked at him. Shock filled her face as she saw him standing there at the door, drunk and mean. "Go away, cat! The cat lover ain't here no more!" Then he threw his nearly empty whiskey bottle at her. It shattered right in front of her, and as she ran away; scared, she knew he would be no help to her. In fact she made a mental note; if she ever became human again she would throw him out of her house and her life the same way he did to her just now.

But that was a week ago and not much had happened since then. She went back to the city, snooping around the crime scene where she had last been seen, trying to find clues as to how she got this way but she had no luck. Finally with no hope, a new-found desperation and the feeling of near starvation she was just about ready to give up. She had looked at herself for the last time she thought to herself as she walked away from the darkened store window and faced the street. She was ready to end it all the only way she knew how, when her feline senses caught a gust of wind carrying a familiar smell. Suddenly a new feeling swept over her and she felt the new found excitement to live. She raced to the alley where the smell was coming from and spotted a scrumptious half eaten carcass of fish laying enticingly on the ground next to a couple of beat up trash cans. It was like God had placed it there for her. Like he had given her a reason to live, to re-nourish her body and continue on with her trek to find the truth.

So with no one around, and no dangers a brew, she pounced upon her dinner. The juices of the fish made her taste buds water, and she planned to enjoy this fish as if it was her last. Who knows it could very well be she thought to herself. She sat down in front of her makeshift dining-room, curled her tail up beside her left arm, placed a light brown paw upon one end of the fish and started to consume her dinner. Immediately she felt the nutrients engage her body, immediately she felt her energy pick up.

Yet only a moment passed when a gang of alley cats strolled up the alley following the same scrumptious scent as she smelled. Smelling the enticing dish Miss Goldie had in front of her, they did not hesitate. All four alley cats lunged at her throat, determined to snatch the fish away from her. Miss Goldie was starving. She hadn't eaten in days, and now had found the determination to not only keep her dinner, but to teach these vicious cats a lesson. Seeing the cats racing towards her she clutched the fish in her mouth as tight as she could and ran. In one mad dash she had pulled away from the pursuing cats and was racing full speed ahead out of the alley. It did not take long before the alley cats had caught up to Miss Goldie, though she out maneuvered them each time they tried to close in on her.

Noticing a large amount of rubble ahead, Miss

Goldie scurried over it into an alley, hoping to find some sort of hideout, or at least an exit, but there was only a tall brick wall blocking her path. She hurriedly tried to figure out a solution to her problem, but it was too late, there was rustling behind her, and she knew instantly who was there. She held that fish tightly in her jaws. There was a sense of pure determination in her to keep this fish and she would stop at nothing to do so. To her, it felt like her last chance. If she lost this fish, she would have lost the fight for life.

Using every ounce of strength she had left to out run these felines, she knew without the nourishment this fish would provide, she would surely be too weak to go on. She wasted no time at all finding a way out of her predicament, thanks to the absorbed knowledge from old movies she used to watch as a human; she leapt on top of a dumpster behind her with all of her might, narrowly missed the teeth of one of the alley cats. Then taking another leap of faith on top of an unsteady pile of crates just tall enough to get her over the brick wall, she leapt over the blockade to freedom, the fish tightly grasped within her mouth. Her powerful hind legs were strong enough to get her over the fence, and knock over the crates, making an avalanche of wood falling at the cowering cats below. Goldie landed safely on the other side with her dinner safe in tow.

Once Goldie had cleared the brick obstacle, she didn't dare look back. If the cats were still after her, there was no reason to stop and find out. She just held onto that fish with all of her might and ran as fast as her paws could take her. After what seemed like a mile she started to slow down. She was getting tired, and she hadn't heard anyone following her so she stopped and checked. When she saw no one pursuing her she gave a sigh of relief, and relaxed. The juices of the fish dripping from her mouth, made her realize her determination had paid off. She had won her fish fair and square and looked forward to enjoying it now in peace.

Yet right at that moment she heard a loud, familiar noise, an unmistakable and scary noise, the sound of a siren bellowing closer and closer towards her. She swung her head around, only to be blinded by two bright lights growing larger every second. Frozen with absolute fear, her mouth opened and she dropped her prize fish onto the ground. The extreme terror that filled her body was all she had left of her soul when Miss Goldie saw her life flash in front of her eyes.

The sounds of skidding tires were the only things that filled the night air as the end of a life escaped our universe.

Chapter 2

As night came about, the sun set in the distance discoloring the house with that warm orange glow that always made the evening feel warm and welcoming. The kids raced through the house playfully, wearing off their homemade cherry pie dessert they had eaten a few hours earlier. Playing hide and go seek, they laughed and giggled each time the other was found and those sounds of laughter filled her heart tremendously. As the cuckoo clock chimed eight thirty though, she knew the hard part was fast approaching. As she slowly rose from her soft recliner, she stretched, took a long deep breath and sighed with a smile. Then she walked up the stairs to the children's room and prepared for the arguments she was about to receive.

"It's time for bed kids."

"Ah Grandma, do we gotta?"

She smiled. They were so sweet and so cute. Little Johnny was eight and three quarters and little Jenny was seven. Already dressed in their night clothes, Jenny in a white lace gown that made her look like an angel holding a soft white teddy bear, Johnny in camouflage cotton, he looked like a warrior and the empty paper towel roll he held like a sword simply fit the theory perfectly.

"It's nearly bed time."

They hemmed and hawed but begrudgingly crawled into their beds. As Grandma was tucking them in though a question arose.

"Grandma, tell us a story."

"Yeah, tell us a love story!" Jenny piped up. Johnny grumbled at that wanting to hear a story with action and adventure instead. Seeing his pout, a thought came to Grandma's mind.

"Actually kids, I do have a story. It's a wonderful love story, true love..." Jenny smiled brightly as Johnny scowled, "but there is a lot of action, near death experiences and a brave hero."

Johnny perked up. "Cool, Grandma. Tell us the story!"

"Please!!!" They both sang in unison.

"Alright." She smiled as she settled down on the bed next to Jenny and took a deep breath attempting to remember the best place to start the story.

"A long, long time ago... a time before hand held computers, Blue Ray disks and video games..."

"Wow that WAS a long time ago!" Johnny spoke.

She smiled, put a finger in front of her mouth, to keep Johnny quiet and then continued. "It began on a night, very much like tonight."

Darkness covered the room. The perfect rhythm of stomping feet, clapping hands, and beating drums packed the auditorium. One musical note grew gradually louder, like a locomotive barreling down the railway. Then finally, at the loudest moment, flash went the lights, exposing an enormous crowd of energy, screaming through the building like the bursting of a atom bomb. The beat grew wildly fast, as the pom-pom's raised to the roof. Leaping into the air with a victorious cheer, the cheerleaders ran, flipped, and tumbled onto the gym floor. The school band was rocking the place out, the students were screaming and cheering, and the football players, fought their way to the middle of the stadium to take their bows for a job well done on the field tonight. The victory game had been won by a landslide and this pep rally was just the beginning of what would be an amazing party through the night.

It was the last game of their last year of college and as the group stood; their cheering and whooping of excitement with the rest of the auditorium; the knowledge of what was to come ahead was swimming in their heads. The uncertainty of the future picked at their hearts but they knew no matter what happened, no matter what obstacles came their way, they all would be friends forever, and nothing, absolutely nothing would ever change that.

"Best friends forever!" Little Jenny chimed in catching her grandmother off guard. She looked at the little girl with a smile and with a finger over her mouth, she shushed the girl and then began to resume her story. She was just about to pick up where she left off when something occurred to her.

"Oh my, I started a little too soon. I should go back a bit and tell you how they all met." The grandmother realized. She took a deep breath going further back in the story, Johnny shifted in his bed wondering when the action would begin.

The day Ally met Jim was nothing special. It was Ally's first day at that high school and Jim was completely preoccupied with the game that afternoon to pay attention to class, muchless the new girl, although thinking back he could have kicked himself for not paying attention when she walked through that door.

That morning at the Prairie Dust High School everyone celebrated together in a pep rally that was meant to rally the excitement of the students and exemplify the encouragement of the players. It was the first game of the season, the players had practiced hard all summer long and tonight they were going to prove to the school that their hard work was going to pay off with a glorious win against their rivals.

As the new girl entered the hallways of the school she found them oddly empty. Worried at first that she was late for class she checked her schedule, her watch and then a nearby classroom. Once certain she wasn't late for class she looked around and investigated the place swiftly making her way towards the school gym and the sound of cheering and music. When she walked through the door she felt the excitement of the crowd rush over her. Everything felt so hyper she couldn't help but smile with enthusiasm. Not aware that her entrance had attracted attention, she continued to walk towards the bleachers and an empty spot up front to watch the rally.

Placing her leather bound books on the floor next to her, she fixed the skirt of her light blue checked dress with white lace trim and swept her flowing brown hair from her shoulder. She then watched the action of the floor for a moment until the band changed music and she watched as everyone stood at attention. Catching on that this must have been the school's fight song she too stood and looked around the gymnasium at the students in the bleachers.

Feeling that not a single eye was on her she relaxed a bit, taking note of the clothing styles the girls were wearing, the hair styles, all so proper, the dresses just below the knee, a single strand of pearls around the neck, the perfect 1950s do. The first day at a new school in a new town, determined to make the best of it, determined to make friends, she was slightly worry that she might not fit in, but that would never stop her from trying.

When the song ended and everyone began cheering, the principal of the school approached the makeshift podium and announced everyone's dismissal along with wishing everyone a good day at school. As the crowd of students began their descent from the upper bleachers towards Allison she scrambled to gather her books but one was knocked under the bleachers before she could reach it. Scrambling through the crowd and to the side opening of the bleachers she made her way underneath and began searching for her book. Spotting it, then reaching for it she overheard the drawl of a female student speak to her group of friends.

“Anyone see that new girl?”

“Blue dress?”

“Yeah that's the one – what do we know about her?”

The other girls shrugged as they continued with the flow of the crowd out of the gymnasium. Allison learned one thing that moment, her arrival hadn't been unnoticed.

“Grandma! The story's about a girl in high school?” Johnny interrupted with a whine and a gurgle of the 'r' as he groaned the word girl.

“Yes Johnny. The story is about a girl but high school is where it begins, not where it ends.”

“When does the life and death stuff start happening? When does the hero come?”

“Soon Johnny, but you have to get to know all of the main characters first and that's why I started here.”

“How much longer until we get to the good stuff?”

“Johnny.” the grandmother scowled and

Johnny quieted and apologized. "Sorry Grandma, you can keep going."

"Thank you. Now where was I?"

"The girl was under the bleachers and the other girls were talking about her." Jenny perked up excited to be of help. Grandma smiled brightly at Jenny then continued her story.

So the gossip began.

As Allison made her way through the now crowded hallway to her first class she was even more curious as to how this day was going to go. As the bell rang and class began the teacher stood with her attendance register and called roll, noticing the new student's name she asked Allison to stand and introduce herself.

Allison stood and shyly looked around the room at the eyes that were staring at her and quickly spoke. "My names Allison, my friends call me Ally, I just moved here from Memphis."

"Memphis huh? Do you know Elvis?" One of the girls asked but the teacher interrupted her.

"You all can ask your questions after class. Right now we have a pop quiz."

Everyone groaned as Ally sat back down and she too took out pencil and paper for the test.

That day was rather dull, I'll admit. Making friends is not always the easiest thing to do when you are new, but one of the key things of that day is that after school, Ally joined the journalism department.

That was the day she met Joyce Olsen, and Joyce and she were soon to become best friends. Being paired to do a major story with differing aspects of the situation really brought the two of them together, although they didn't agree with each other for a good while but when their story came together, they realized how great of a team they made. Joyce was the one who took Ally under her wing and introduced her to everyone she knew.

The next really good friend Ally made was Cindy, and oh was Cindy a handful. Cindy knew when she was five years old that she wanted to be a movie star and she never once faltered from that dream. Cindy was in every school play, joined the drama department the very first chance she got, and by the end of high school was volunteering at the local news station; trying to learn everything she could about the world of media before she went out to Hollywood for her big chance.

"Did Cindy become a movie star?" Jenny spoke up, completely excited at the idea of a Hollywood actress."

"You'll have to wait until I get there sweetie. Now, no more interruptions from either of you."

"Yes Grandma."

Ally met Cindy one day in the lunch-line. Cindy was grabbing the same brownie as Ally was reaching for. Cindy let Ally have it, but when they met for the second time, reaching for the same milk carton, Cindy and Ally began to laugh. They sat together during lunch, and by the end of the lunch hour, Ally and Cindy had found dozens of things they had in common, along with the fact that Cindy lived only two houses down from Ally. Ally introduced Joyce to Cindy and from then on, the three of them became life long sisters.

A couple of months later, while hanging out at the Burger Shack, the three of them were discussing what to wear to the Fall Formal when Ally finally met Jim officially. Cindy and Joyce already had dates and they were scheming to find Ally a date but little did they know that was about to be taken care of for them. As a couple of the athletes from high school entered the diner they saw Jim sitting at a booth one down from Ally and her friends. Jim was just taking a bite of hamburger when one of the guys spoke a quick "think fast" and threw a football at Jim. With not enough time to react; to drop the hamburger and catch the ball, he ducked and the ball flew over his head and landed on the table behind him knocking over Ally's drink.

"Cool!" Johnny interrupted sitting up in his bed "Did she get soaked?"

Grandma scowled at him and he laid back

down.

Ally on the other hand saw the ball coming and anticipated Jim's non-reaction, when the ball hit the table, she leapt from her seat moments before the drink splashed all over her chair. Spinning in his chair with mouth full of food, Jim noticed how quickly Ally had reacted and as he scrambled to swallow his bite, the other two athletes ran up to apologize for spilling her drink. She nonchalantly excused their behavior when Jim approached and personally apologized.

"Sorry about that, let me buy you a new drink."

"Be my guest."

"Pretty good reaction time there. If you were a guy I'd be worried about my spot on the team."

"Lucky for you then." Ally smiled coyly.

Jim smiled at that. They struck up a conversation and the rest is history.

"Grandma, pleeeease tell me that's not the end of the story!" Johnny groaned. He had been sitting there patiently all this time waiting for the action and was increasingly loosing patience when he heard what sounded to be a finalizing of the story just now.

"Is it just getting interesting?" Grandma questioned.

"No! It's been boring so far. When do you get to the excitement?"

"It's coming up. I promise."

Jim and Ally struck up a conversation that day that Jim wanted to continue later, he suggested Friday night and Ally graciously accepted. However when Friday night came about it turned out to be a horrible evening. It was storming outside, lightning and thunder, there was flash flooding. The wind wasn't just whistling through the leaves of the trees, it was screaming at the top of its lungs blowing over trees, ripping through the eaves of the roof. The rain was pounding against the fragile glass window like pebbles being thrown out of a pitcher's hand. The lightning was streaking across the sky and the thunder was so incredibly loud it was like a concert loud and terrifying yet exciting.

Ally sat in her window shivering at each loud boom of the thunder, staring out the window watching desperately to see if Jim was on the way.

All dressed up and ready to go on their date, Ally wasn't sure if she wanted to go anywhere in this weather. She just hoped Jim was okay. He was supposed to be there at 6:30 and it was now fast approaching 8pm. There was only two excuses she could think of for him to be late; he's either lost, although she thought she gave him great directions, or else the weather has held him up. She tried not to be a pessimist until nine-o-clock with no phone call, and then she'd start to think he forgot about her. She didn't want to even consider he might have been in an accident because she didn't want to consider anything bad happening to him.

The thunder sure was loud as it sounded in the night sky and each time it rang a loud boom she'd shudder. Jim said he drove a white pick-up, so that's what she was looking for when a set of headlights turned onto her street. Ally kept a watch on him as he pulled up her driveway, and got out of his truck. He just got out of his truck and he looked like he was already soaked to the bone. Noticing this, she went to get a towel for him and met him at the front door.

Jim walked up to the door, dripping wet, his dark brown hair, dripping down his face. He rang the doorbell, and a moment later an angel opened the door.

"Want a towel?" She began before even saying hello.

"Thanks." He said as he graciously took the towel and wiped his face.

"So what happened to you?"

"I got a flat tire coming off the main road, that's why I'm late. The wind not only knocked the umbrella out of my hands, it also knocked my truck off the jack, so I had to crawl in the mud under the truck to get the jack back, and set it up again. By the time I was done, I was soaked, covered in mud, and ready to just go home, but I thought since this was our first date, I'd still come over and at least explain why I didn't show up on time in person. You don't mind if I cancel our date now, do you? I wouldn't want you to go out with me when I'm all muddy."

He looked so disappointed, and yet Ally loved how he felt so strongly about getting to her, that he went through all of that just to cancel their date. Well, of course she wouldn't send him home after all of that. She invited him inside, brought him her dad's bathrobe and insisted on washing his clothes. She then fixed grilled cheese sandwiches, and they watched TV. It wasn't like going out to a restaurant, but it was definitely cozy. By about ten-thirty his clothes were done, the show was over, and Ally's father had gone to bed. Ally felt that the end of their first date was coming to an end and they hadn't even talked about the dance yet. She went into the kitchen to clean up the dishes while Jim got dressed, then he came into the kitchen to join her.

"I had a wonderful time tonight Ally, you make the world's greatest grilled cheese."

"Thanks, it was my mother's recipe."

He stood there, grabbed a towel and began drying the dishes that she had just washed.

"Jim, you don't have to do that."

"Sure I do. I canceled our first date, you ended up cooking and doing the dishes, it's only fair that I dry, and that I ask you to go with me on a second attempt first date, next Friday."

"Next Friday is the Fall Formal Dance." Ally said shocked that he didn't seem to remember.

"Are you going with anybody yet?"

"No."

"Well then, do you want to go with me?"

Jim said the words Ally had been waiting for

all night, and she wasted no time in her answer,

"Yes, I'd love to go with you."

"Well, then it's settled."

He had such a big smile on his face, like he had just won the grand prize sweepstakes, and Ally couldn't help but know she was beaming as well. Ally then walked him to the door, and then the second part of the date she'd been waiting for all night long happened, they kissed goodnight. It was such a nice kiss, delicate and gentle yet powerful and wonderful all at the same time. She watched him get into his truck and drive off, then she ran upstairs to write about it in her journal.

Grandma peered over at Johnny who was playing the gag me sign with his finger in his mouth, but when he saw his grandmother looking at him he stopped. Realizing she needed to get to the 'good part' soon she decided to jump back to the last day of college and pick up the story there.

Chapter 3

"Alright kids, now we'll get to the exciting part of the story."

"Good!" Johnny piped in but Jenny wasn't quite ready.

"Do Ally & Jim go to the dance? Do they have a good time?"

"Oh yes. They had an amazing time, and they kept seeing each other through high school, they all ended up going to the same college, Ally, Jim, Joyce, even Cindy who really wanted to go straight to Hollywood but her parents insisted on a proper education and when she discovered the drama department was connected to the towns theatrical society and that she'd be able to get real-life experience on stage she was really excited about that."

"Did she ever go to Hollywood Grandma?"

"You'll have to wait and find out.

"But there is a hero right?" Johnny questioned again.

"Yes Johnny, there is a hero. But first, there needs to be a reason to call for a hero." Grandma egged as Johnny rubbed his hands together eagerly waiting for this part.

It was their last night in college. The tests were done, the grades were out, the future plans had been made. All that was left for the graduating class to do was to celebrate, and tonight, was all about celebration.

A large group had gone out to Miller's Bluff; a beautiful place at night, especially on a full moon. There's this large pasture, a huge open field that surrounds a great lagoon with a waterfall. The pasture is blocked by a good size hill, about fifty to seventy-five feet high where a stream ends into the waterfall. It's very romantic. The sound of rushing water, the reflection of the moon off the moving water makes the entire pasture shimmer like glitter. And near the group they had created a couple of campfires and some of the vehicles had their radios turned to the same station, so there was music and laughter and joy. It was a perfect night.

Jim and Ally walked up the hill to a nice secluded spot where Jim again professed his love to Ally.

“Ally you are an amazing woman. I thank God every day for introducing us.” Ally smiled as Jim continued. “Would you marry me?” He asked as he pulled out a ring box. Ally's eyes began to tear up as Jim opened the box and the evenings moonbeams refracted off of the diamond. Ally graciously accepted and kissed Jim.

"Oh God! They're not going to make out are they?" Johnny interrupted again with exasperation.

Grandma smiled, knowing that boys will be boys and that at least she was keeping Johnny's attention, she continued.

The night was warm. Many of the kids from the group were swimming in the lagoon, there was drinking, some of the cooler guys would jump off of the cliff from the waterfall and land in the deep end of the lagoon. The girls would just swoon over them, how cool, how brave, and of course, the more they drank, the crazier their stunts became. Jim and Ally were in the shadows kissing when a group of real show-offs came up to jump off the cliff. They were drunk and loud and their conversation carried over to the two love birds.

"Hey man, anyone cast an eyeball at that blonde bombshell down there?"

"The one in the green halter top and pigtails?"

"Yeah I could totally yank those."

"Yeah, she's totally stacked."

Ally knew that Cindy was wearing a green halter top and she had just recently started wearing her hair in pigtails but she wasn't sure if these guys were talking about Cindy or not, although their conversation about her became more lude as they continued it.

"I'd love to rack those, if you get my drift?"

"What a classy chassis."

By now Jim had heard enough. Ally didn't need to hear these guys comments and he was fairly certain they were discussing Cindy as well and before Ally knew what was going on; Jim was already heading towards the group addressing them.

"Hey guys I think you ought to cool it about the chick.

"What's it to you daddy-o?"

"I think your talking about a friend of mine and I'm not hip to it."

"Well I think you need to wail on someone else's party man. Get bent!"

"I'm not looking for a pounding, but I suggest you guys cut it out."

"Well I think this guys lookin' for a bruisin'"

"Maybe a knuckle sandwich."

By now Ally had heard enough, afraid for what would happen to Jim, one to four. Ally ran up to stop Jim. "Come on baby, lets just leave."

"Yeah baby, listen to dolly." One of the guys egged on.

"Ally walk away." Jim pressed as the four guys began their forward assault. But Ally didn't want to see anyone fight. As one guy threw a punch and another grabbed for a nearby stick, Ally ran in the middle of the fight. However one of the guys, pushed Ally away and when he touched her Jim blew his cool. He jumped into that group of guys fists blazin' which when Ally saw this she became even more worried about Jim. When she ran back to him he was just receiving a massive blow to the chin and when he stumbled backwards, he bumped into Ally hard which made her loose her balance.

When all five guys noticed that Ally was stumbling and how close she was to the edge of the cliff, their thinking switched and as they watched her in what seemed to be slow motion loose her footing and teeter over the edge of the cliff, screaming, Jim leapt to his feet as fast as he could and ran towards her. But just as he reached for her hand gravity pulled her over and he fell to the ground, peering over the edge as he watched Ally falling.

After that everything seemed to slow down. She saw the fear on his face so detailed as she looked up from her fall. He was so scared and so sad, she could almost see his heart breaking through his facial expressions. She saw the drunk guys looking over the edge with complete shock on their face, an empty whiskey bottle still tightly grasped in one guys hand. Then she turned, tumbling in the air, now facing the water, fast approaching, she saw her reflection in the shallow water getting closer and closer. Her scream grew hoarse, almost like a growl. Then it happened. Ally saw her reflection in the mirror-like lake change. She saw weird things happening. She looked at her hands, they looked like they were shrinking, and for a second she thought she was losing her mind. That the fear and near death experience was playing tricks on her. But hair, no, fur was growing on her hands, soft golden fur. She felt sick inside, she was screaming for help, but everything sounded like a cat's scream. Was she turning into a cat? She must have been hallucinating, because after that she blacked out.

Jim watched as his love fell to her doom. There was nothing he could do. Nothing anybody could do. However, he couldn't quite believe what he was seeing ether. He saw her arms and legs shrinking, he saw her body turn small and furry, he saw a golden cats tail protrude out of her buttocks. Within mere seconds after a bright flash of light, Jim saw his precious Ally transform from a living woman, into a cat, not falling to her death, but twisting around in the open air like a small speck of dust searching for the perfect place to land. Then finally, ready and waiting to land on all fours, she did.

Ally the cat landed ferociously fast on a hard rock that protruded from the far left edge of the lagoon, then bounced back up from the velocity of pressure and then landed once again on her side in the water knocked out from the shock and quickly beginning to sink. As Jim's eyes focused on the creature which nearly instantly transformed back into Ally, Jim found the courage to leap from the cliff himself, aiming right to avoid the rock and try to hit the deep end. As he dove into the water, many kids from the shore were intently watching; had heard the commotion and screams moments earlier; had watched Ally fall from the cliffs edge; had seen something weird happen but couldn't for the life of themselves believe what they actually saw, and as they neared the shoreline, waiting with bated breath to see if Jim emerged from the water and to see if he had Ally in his arms; the night grew silent. Cindy and Joyce ran up to the shoreline, all were holding their breath, including the four guys looking down from the top of the cliff, panic-stricken.

The time ticked by slower than molasses, you could have heard a pin drop as everyone waited with bated breath, then finally, what seemed like absolutely forever, Jim shot up out of the water, Ally’s limp body grasped tightly in his arms. As soon as some of the guys from the shoreline saw the two of them they jumped into the water to help bring the two to land. Ally was out cold, and a voice could be heard calling for anyone who could do CPR. Ally's body was dragged onto the shoreline, some people crowded, others backed away to give space. One of the guys from the medical department came running up and immediately began CPR as Joyce and Cindy went to Jim with towels and tried to inquire as to what happened.

Jim, on the other hand, was out of breath exhausted and beside himself with worry. Ally still wasn't breathing and as the seconds ticked by like minutes, Jim's worry increased. His heart was beating rapidly, every muscle in his body was tense and as he watched the med student continue compressions on Ally's chest and breathe into her mouth, Jim's knees began to tremble. As he fell to his knees, and Joyce began to feel the tears filling her eyes and the murmurs began quietly around the crowd, Ally gasped for her first breath.

"Oh thank God! She's okay!" Johnny exclaimed with so much conviction it made his grandmother burst into laughter.

Jenny on the other hand was exploding with curiosity, "Did she really turn into a cat? Grandma, did anyone record it?"

Grandma looked at her sweet granddaughter and smiled, "Remember this was long before digital cameras and video recorders. Long before cell phones and laptops too." She watched as Jenny moped a bit and then looked forward to the next part, certain about this even though it hadn't been said yet. "But someone did get pictures."

"They did?" Johnny questioned curiously wondering when he missed that.

Grandma smiled and slid her finger under Jenny's chin to show her how proud she was, then continued the story.

When the four boys at the top of the cliff saw Ally move they realized she was going to be okay, then in their drunken state one said "We should split." Which the other three quickly agreed with.

As Ally sat up and a couple nearby girls brought her towels and the guys were pushed back as the inquiries began, Jim, Joyce and Cindy pressed their way in to check on Ally themselves. Jim was in full-protection mode as he kept asking, "Are you alright? Are you hurt? Is anything broken?"

He was feeling around Ally's arms, wrists,

legs, she touched her side and he quickly inquired about her ribs, “I'm fine!” Ally finally spoke.

“Wiggle your fingers.”

“Wiggle your toes.” came the helpful suggestions of the crowd. Ally couldn't even tell who was speaking, there were so many faces. Confusion set in as Joyce pressed in to see her friend and as Ally began to try to get to her feet, to regain some control of her surroundings, Joyce felt an arm on her shoulder.

As Joyce turned to see a fellow student from the journalism department, she heard Ally again exclaim that she was fine, but Joyce could see the eyes of her fellow journalist, Brad, and knew there was something important he needed to talk to her about. As she followed him out of the crowd curiously, he led her to a nearby tree and carefully chose his words.

“Brad, what's up?”

“I was playing with the schools camera. I had been taking a few stills of the party, and then was working on my night technique, trying to get some good pictures of the moonlight reflecting off of the waterfall when we all heard the scream. Actually, I had zoomed in and saw the fight up on the cliff.”

“Did you get pictures of the attackers?”

“Yes, but that's not the whole reason I got you out here. Did you see her fall?”

“Yeah, kind of. When I heard the scream I looked that way but it happened so quick.”

“Did you see the cat?”

“What cat?”

Brad paused, not wanting to sound insane, he needed to develop his film before he could really prove what he was about to say. “I was clicking pictures of her as she fell. I'm not sure how they'll turn out since she was moving and I was zoomed in... you didn't see the cat?”

“What cat Brad?”

“Did it look like she turned into a cat when she fell?” He asked so carefully he almost cringed at the words coming out of his mouth.

Joyce stared at him.

“I know what that sounds like, but think back a bit, when you were watching her fall, did anything look weird?”

“My best friend Ally was falling, the entire scenario looked weird.”

“So you didn't see it?”

Joyce paused. She pulled the recent memory of the event back into her head even though it was quite traumatic and tried to slow it down. As she did, her eyes looked back up at Brad, widened, her brow furrowed. As her mouth opened just slightly Brad got the response he was looking for.

“Would you like to be with me as I develop these pictures?”

Staring at him, her own mind obviously playing tricks on her, a journalists curiosity got the better of her. “Yes.”

Awesome!” Little Johnny declared, “She's a

shape shifter!"

"Johnny stop interrupting the story!" Jenny scolded him.

"That's okay Jenny," Grandma interjected, "This is a good spot to stop for the night."

"But you can't stop now! It's just getting good!" Johnny bellowed.

"It's time for bed now. I'll tell you more about Ally tomorrow."

"Promise?"

"Promise." Grandma said as she pulled the covers under Jenny's chin and kissed her on the forehead. When she turned to Johnny he was sitting on the top of his covers bouncing.

"Grandma, you can't stop it there. I have to know what happened."

"So I guess the story isn't boring anymore?"

"Well yeah it was, but it's just getting good."

"Then maybe tomorrow night, you won't interrupt me so much and I can tell you more."

"Yes Grandma." He sighed with a mope.

"Goodnight dear."

Chapter 4

The next morning when the grand kids woke up they jumped right into play mode, all but forgetting the story. They got dressed and went to breakfast and never once inquired about Ally the cat. The day was half over when Jenny ran inside for a good hiding place, when she saw her grandmother sitting on the couch with her pet cat in her lap. Suddenly the story popped into her head and she wondered if she could hear more of it.

"Grandma, can you tell me more of that story?"

"What story dear?"

"The story of the girl and the waterfall and the cat." She sat down next to her Grandma and the cat stood up and stretched, then walked towards her expecting to be petted. As she reached for the cat Johnny came running inside.

"Ready or not... hey, you're not hiding!"

"I want to hear more about the story." Jenny quickly answered. As the cat circled her lap and prepared to lay down, Johnny ran up.

"Grandma, you going to tell us more?"

"I wasn't planning on it..." she paused seeing the pouts begin to form, "but I could. If you really want me to."

"Oh yes we do!" They both declared in unison.

"Okay then." She inhaled, "where was I?"

"Ally just woke up." "The guy was going to print the pictures." Both children spoke together. The grandmother smiled as she knew she had the kids hooked.

Ally and Jim were sitting in Jim's car just outside of the dorms talking that night when Jim had to get something off of his chest. The events of that night were ripe in his mind and they kept playing over and over again like a chipped record.

"I have to tell you something. I have to get this off of my chest."

"Of course baby, what is it?"

He took a deep breath and closed his eyes. "I went temporarily insane when I was watching you fall away from me." He admitted.

"How do you mean Jim?"

"My eyes started playing tricks with me. I swear I watched you turn into a cat and land on all four paws but I know that sounds insane."

Ally had all but blocked out that very vivid, very insane memory as well when she was falling determined to believe it was stress but when Jim mentioned it just now, her heart skipped a beat. Not wanting to think about it, or admit she was crazy or worse yet a freak she changed the subject. Leaning on Jim's shoulder she pulled up her left hand and let the engagement ring glisten in the moonlight.

"Maybe you're having cold feet?"

Jim immediately forgot the previous moment and dove feet first into this moment. He pulled Ally into his arms and kissed her. When he pulled away, just inches, he spoke, "Never."

On the other side of town, in a very empty journalism room, Joyce and Brad made their way back to the dark room. Joyce didn't know Brad well personally but knew that his name appeared under many of the pictures in the schools newspaper. As he flicked on the red light and pulled out his photograph processing chemicals, Joyce closed the door behind her and watched with anticipation.

The task was long and daunting, and as she watched she didn't know what Brad was doing, first he'd place a thick paper in one container of solution, then place it in the next, then hang it to dry. He did this for dozens of pictures and as Joyce watched, she kept looking over at the white pages hanging on the clothes line and witnessed as images appeared on the paper. It was quite magical as the images formed and when they were all done, and after Brad had finished putting his things away, he flicked on the lights and pulled the finished pages down and placed them on the counter.

Joyce watched with extreme curiosity as he flipped through some party shots and then slowed when he got to the waterfall. When he got to the one of the fight at the top of the hill, he placed it to his right and Joyce picked it up to take a closer look to see if she recognized the guys. She was focused on that when Brad interrupted her train of thought with a gasp.

"Oh my God."

Joyce placed the photograph on the counter and focused her attention on the picture in Brad's hands. It was blurry, he had been moving the camera downwards, following the fall, the background was blurry the foreground was streaked but mixed in with the various grays of the water, the darker grays of the grass bordering the frame of the picture, and the gray rock protruding from the water was a small lighter grey figure that resembled a feline, with paws stretched downwards and tail stretched up. Joyce focused on it for just a moment when the picture previous caught her attention and she could just barely make out her friend, half on the blurry photograph half off. Recognizing her best friend, seeing in print that moment where she was falling, the realization came to her that her friend nearly died tonight and she choked back a tear. Realizing now that she hadn't even talked to Ally afterward she completely forgot the reason she was even standing here when Jim brought her back to the task at hand.

"Do you see this?" What does this look like?"

Joyce peered back at the photograph in Brads hands and shook her head. "It's blurry."

"Yeah it's blurry, I was moving the camera following a moving object in the dark, but there," he pointed, "what does that look like to you?"

"She's not an object, she's my best friend."

"It's a cat. I'm telling you, it's a cat."

"It's impossible!"

Brad threw down the picture and quickly

shoved the pictures outwards onto the counter putting them in order. “Look at this. You watched me pull the film, you watched me develop it. This is what I took in order. The fight, the falling from the edge, this one doesn't have anything but the waterfall because I didn't follow her down, but I caught up with her on this one, and that one she's half off the page but you can still see the form of a human, yes it's blurry but you can see her arms and torso, and then this one just a few feet further down but the figure is nothing like a human, it's almost smaller and doesn't that look like a tail?”

Joyce picked up the photograph that came next, it was less blurry but showed the splash of the water as Ally went in. She stared at that one, then back at the one in Brad's hand. Then she peered at the one to his left, the one right before that had half of her body off of the page, then back to the one in Brad's hand. She switched her focus from one picture to the next a few more times, each time spending a few more moments on the one in Brad's hand until she couldn't take her eyes off of it, and then she turned her back and put her hand over her eyes.

“You see it don't you?”

“I don't know what I see.”

“You see it.”

There was silence in the room for a long few moments when Brad spoke up. “This is going to be worth a fortune.”

Going over the nights events in his head, Jim tossed and turned all night. Bumping into Ally, making her loose her balance, turning and reaching for her only to watch her slip away, he kept waking in terror. Realizing it was just a dream, he attempted to get back to sleep again, but each time he closed his eyes, all he could see was Ally falling from him, the look of terror on her face as she reached upwards towards him while falling further away.

Jim tried to get past that moment but his mind just wouldn't cooperate. As he watched Ally falling farther and farther away from him he knew his eyes had played tricks on him. Watching her twirl in the air as she continued to fall, watching her back arch as she braced for landing, watching the cat land on all fours...

Jim shot up from bed, awake again and sweating, he shook his head. “It was just my eyes playing tricks on me.” He laid his head back on his extremely wet pillow and closed his eyes again, there she was, her eyes looking at him, her hand reached towards him, her scream calling out into the night air like a cats cry.

Jim woke again. He felt he was going insane. He knew that tonight's activities had put a great deal of stress on him. That this was his brains way of figuring out what he had been through and helping him to cope, but how was this helping? How is seeing Ally transform into a cat helping him not to be insane? Throwing the covers off of his body, he stood from bed and began pacing the room talking to himself.

"It's just a dream. It didn't really happen. I'm simply going nuts. It was too much stress for me to handle. That's all, too much stress." He had once again convinced himself and was just about to go back to bed when he heard a knock at the door. Peering over at the clock on his bed side table, he scrunched his eyes to make out the hour and minute hand and when he realized it was two in the morning he wasn't sure who to expect at the door.

When he opened the door he was shocked to see Joyce standing there. He was trying to come up with a smart-aleck remark when he noticed the look on her face and the fact that she was upset and he quickly asked her to come inside.

"I'm sorry to show up here at such an hour but when I saw your bedroom light was on..."

"Are you okay? What's going on?"

Joyce took a deep breath, trying still as she had all night, to figure out how to tell him this without sounding insane herself when Jim noticed her hands were trembling.

"Are you cold? Should I get you a blanket?"

"Jim I don't know how to tell you this. I really don't know how to say this without completely freaking you out."

"Just say it." He spoke completely perplexed as to what Joyce was so upset about.

She exhaled and then just jumped right into it as fast as she possibly could in hopes of dulling the pain. "After Ally fell, Brad Johnson pulled me aside and told me something I still can't quite believe but to prove what he was saying we went to the darkroom at the journalism department and developed the pictures he took with his camera and although they were really blurry because she was falling and he was moving the camera, it really did look like her in one picture and a cat in the next and now Brad is talking about selling the story to the news crews and gathering other eye-witnesses and I really don't know if anyone will believe him but I thought you should know because Ally's been through so much already and..."

Hold up!" Jim spoke loudly while holding up his hands. "Catch your breath, and go over this thing a bit slower – Brad got pictures?"

"Yeah and now he's talking about selling them to the highest bidder."

"Slow down damn it!" Jim spoke harshly trying desperately to catch up. "Brad got pictures of Ally turning into a cat?"

"It's just the one image and it's blurry but it really does look like a cat and I watched him develop them."

"He thinks Ally turned into a cat?"

"Yeah Jim and now he's planning on..."

"Whoa, go back. Did he actually see her turn into a cat?"

"He watched it through the view finder. Why?"

"Did *you* see her turn into a cat?"

"Jim it all happened so quickly..."

"Did you?"

"I don't know what I saw!"

"Has anyone else said anything about it?"

"Jim, you're freaking me out. Did you see her turn into a cat as well?"

"I can't be sure what I saw, but I saw something and I thought it was just in my head that I was seeing things, that the stress was making me nuts, but... if Brad saw it..." Jim began pacing again as Joyce's mouth dropped. "We couldn't both be going nuts right?" Jim turned and looked at Joyce with eager, greedy anticipation, to hear that he wasn't losing it. "Tell me you saw it too. Tell me I'm not nuts."

"You'd rather believe that Ally turned into a cat?" Joyce said with some disgust.

Jim continued to look at her with anticipation when her last words began to ring in his ears. He began shaking his head no even though his face still desired the conclusion that he wasn't going crazy. "Joyce, I keep seeing it. I keep seeing it over and over again every single time I close my eyes. I keep seeing her falling from me, falling away from me and then she turns into a cat and lands on her feet, paws, I don't know! I don't know what to believe! All I know is I can't ignore this information!"

"Well believe this Jim; if Brad gets those pictures out there and someone, anyone believes him, Ally's safety is going to be in question. Your lives together as you know it are over."

"You're right." Jim spoke carefully as he continued to stare at Joyce. It was as if he were waiting for her to tell him what to do next. Joyce sensed that.

"We need to go talk to Brad."

"Right. Good idea." Jim spoke again still staring at Joyce.

He stood there for a few moments longer when Joyce added, "Like now."

"Right!" Jim said as he turned to grab his car keys.

"You may want to change first." Joyce threw in.

Jim stopped and looked down at the clothes he was wearing and realized Joyce was right, confronting Brad about this would be easier if he weren't in his pajamas.

"Brad's gonna get it now" Johnny screeched with delight. Grandma looked at him a bit alarmed and spoke, "Why do you say that?"

"Because the dude's threatening to expose Ally as some shape shifting freak and he can't let that happen."

"Even if it's true?"

"Grandma!" Jenny spoke up shocked, "Is Ally really a shape shifter?"

Grandma smiled sweetly. "I guess you'll find out later."

"Later? Why?" Both kids groaned.

"Because I have to get dinner started." Both kids turned to look at the clock and then whined in unison. As Grandma got up from the couch, her pet cat jumped down and Jenny reached to pet it.

"Grandma will you tell us more tonight?"

"I can do that if you want."

Chapter 5

That night the children were dressed and ready for bed nearly an hour before their bed time. When they were both ready they called down to their grandmother to come up and asked her to tell them more of the story. When she walked into their room and saw the both of them sitting up in bed with excited anticipation she couldn't help but smile. Then she sat down on the bed next to Jenny and smiled, "Where did I leave off?"

"Jim was about to kick Brad's..."

"Johnny!" His Grandma scolded as she interrupted his sentence. Johnny shrunk down a bit and apologized under his breath and looked up at his grandmother with puppy dog eyes waiting to see if she would continue the story. Smiling now, she continued.

So when Jim and Joyce arrived at Brad's dorm room, Joyce wasn't sure what he was planning on doing but got a pretty good idea when Jim didn't even bother knocking on the door but instead kicked it in. Expecting to have startled Brad awake Jim was caught completely off guard when he spotted the guy sitting at his desk, a bunch of crumpled paper on the floor surrounding him.

"Don't hurt me." He spoke with no fear but more with disillusionment.

"I don't want to hurt you I want to see the pictures."

Brad backed away from his desk and got to his feet. "You can't have it. And you can't stop me from selling it."

"Brad I have to see it. I have to know."

"Know what?" Brad questioned curiously.

"I have to see it. I have to know."

"You think you saw her turn too huh?" Brad egged-on.

Jim looked at Brad, his eyes widening as he realized Jim saw it also and he began realizing the ramifications of this picture. "Where's the picture?"

"You're going to destroy it. I know you will."

"Joyce said it was blurry."

"Not too blurry to see the figure."

"Blurry enough that no one would believe you."

"Then why do you look so worried?"

"I'm not, I'm just curious."

"Curious because you saw it too?"

"No, curious as to what it is you think you saw."

Brad realized what was going on here. "It's some place safe. Some place where you'll never find it."

The men were at a stalemate. Jim was trying to determine if he needed to attack and Brad was trying to decide if he should run. Joyce slinked in when Jim's back was to the door and reached down and picked up a couple of the crumpled pieces of paper. As she uncrumpled them the sound grabbed both of their attentions. Jim turned to see what was going on behind him when Brad yelled out, "Don't read those!"

Worried that Brad might attack Joyce, Jim turned his attention back on Brad and demanded that Joyce read the paper.

"What does it say Joyce?"

"It's been scratched out but he was trying to write a letter to the national tabloids about the picture."

"You'd really ruin her life for this story?" Jim growled.

"If it's the truth."

"What if we were just drunk?"

"Pictures don't lie."

"But this one is questionable, right?"

"You need to leave." Brad spoke up beginning to worry.

"Joyce search his desk, find the picture."

"It's not there. I hid it some place safe." Brad insisted as Joyce began opening drawers. When she got to the top left drawer Brad began to freak out. "Stay out of my things!" He said as he began to run towards his desk.

Joyce turned to see Brad coming towards her when Jim grabbed and restrained him. "Keep looking." Jim insisted. Hesitantly Joyce opened the drawer and found an envelope big enough to hold the picture. As she pulled it out of the desk drawer Brad began flailing in Jim's arms.

"Open it!" Jim insisted. Joyce opened the envelope and looked in, seeing the pictures she looked back up at Jim.

"Is it the picture?"

She nodded her head. Brad began flailing more and Jim threw him from his arms, he tumbled over the bed and rolled onto his back on the other side of the room. As he began to get up, Jim yelled, "Stay down!" and as Brad stilled, Jim reached for the pictures and Joyce carefully handed them over.

With a corner of his eye on the now still but anxious Brad, Jim pulled out the pictures and let each one drop to the floor until he came upon the one that stuck out. The one that even though it was blurry, looked like the shape of a cat about to land. He stared at the picture for the longest moment, absorbing the details of the situation, hardly able to comprehend what he was seeing or attempt to figure out how it could be true, how Ally could transform into a cat, when Brad leapt to his feet and began to charge at Jim.

Joyce warned Jim with a scream as she quickly got out of the way and as Brad tackled Jim to the ground and retrieved the picture, jumping to his feet in victory he turned back to prepare for certain attack from Jim when he noticed Jim was still on the floor. Seeing Jim just laying there on the floor seemed weird on so many levels. Joyce moved in closer to make sure Jim hadn't gotten hurt when she and Brad both saw him sitting there staring off into space.

Exchanging glances, reverting their attention back to Jim and then looking back up at each other, Joyce shrugged her shoulder as Brad took a step backwards. Neither of them knew what had to be going through Jim's mind. His girlfriend, now his fiancé, had turned into a cat. How do you get past something like this? How do you address this? A few really long moments passed when Joyce attracted Brad's attention and motioned for the two of them to walk out into the hallway. Reluctantly Brad moved towards the door, afraid at first that Jim would attack him again but when the man didn't move, when he continued to stare off into space, he felt a bit more at ease.

Once in the hallway Joyce turned to Brad and began to speak. "I know that coming in tonight the way we did was wrong but the guy had to know."

"Yeah, yeah I get that."

"I mean his fiancé turned into a cat tonight, he needed to see the proof."

"Right."

"But no one else does." Brad looked at her curiously then almost angrily. She continued. "This picture will do more harm than good. For you and for Ally." Brad started to protest but Joyce continued. "The likelihood that any respectable news organization would believe you is slim to none. The fact that you were trying to write out a letter to the tabloids means you think this too. In the likelihood that you do get the picture and story published with so much doubt your credibility would be shot. Your chance at becoming a well-renowned photographer would go down the drains. And you know it." Brad wanted to protest but he nodded his agreement. "Now, Ally is my best friend, and I love her like a sister. I wouldn't want anything to ever hurt her, and if a story like this came out, true or not, her life would be turned upside down and ruined." Brad listened as Joyce continued. "That being said, I am leaving this up to you. I don't know what Jim's going to do, but between you and me, I say we sit on this story."

Brad's eyes widened as he realized what Joyce was saying.

"The journalist in me wants to get to the truth as well but you can't do that if the story breaks too soon and you are discredited right off the bat." Brad nodded in agreement. "Now this could have been some crazy fluke or we could be in the beginning stages of something absolutely out of this world and between you and me, I'm willing to wait it out and see if this ever happens again. If by the grace of God Ally ever transforms again I want to be ready with camera in hand. I want to be there to figure this thing out. To explain it, to confirm the facts. Are you with me?"

Brad nodded yes when Jim stepped out the door into the hallway. The both of them stared at Jim with worry wondering what he heard, what he was going to say, what he was going to do. They both stared at him as he came out, looking down, putting his thoughts in order, comprehending what he had just heard and then he spoke. "I agree."

Joyce was floored. She hadn't expected a

response like that from Jim and she had absolutely no idea how this thing was going to pan out. As she and Jim left the dorm building together neither one said a word to each other. As Jim drove back to his apartment, the car filled with an eerie silence. When Jim stopped the truck in front of his place, he put it in park then reached for Joyce's hand. At first Joyce felt wrong, like she was doing something immoral but when Jim spoke...

"This is between us. Ally will not find out." He then lifted his hand from her hand and got out of the truck. Nothing more was said, nothing needed to be.

The next morning when Ally woke up she felt oddly well rested. Having had such weird dreams after such a traumatic experience she expected to wake this morning exhausted but she wasn't. As she got dressed, looking forward to the graduation ceremony this afternoon, she thought about the moment Jim proposed. She looked at the ring and smiled, imagined what it would be like to marry him, to be his wife. She thought about the wedding, she thought about the honeymoon, her mind was a million miles away when there was a knock at the door.

Arriving back into reality Ally opened the door and let Cindy inside who was just beaming brighter than she was. Excitement radiated from her pores and Ally could see that Cindy had big news. Cindy pranced inside as Ally closed the door behind her then she turned with a squeal and let it out.

"I've just been offered a role in a big time Hollywood production!" She screamed with excitement as Ally too joined in. As the excitement shot from their bodies they began to jump up and down with delight.

"Cindy that is awesome news!"

"I know! I just had to share it with someone. Can you believe it? Me – in a Hollywood movie!" They squealed some more until their energy ran out and Ally went into the kitchen to get them a bottle of soda.

That afternoon, as the graduating class stood there, anticipating that grand hat throw and the first step into the rest of their life; the friends were deep in thought. Joyce was thinking about her future as a journalist, Brad was thinking about his career as a photographer, Cindy was thinking about her career as a Hollywood actress, Ally was thinking about her life-to-be with Jim and Jim was thinking about....

When Ally came up to him earlier she seemed completely normal. She gave him a kiss and it was wonderful but he felt himself staying oddly indifferent. The situation had changed even though his love for her hadn't and even though she was certain she was going to marry him, Jim wasn't certain about anything anymore. His uncertainty of the future picked at his heart and even though he knew he'd be starting his career as an investigator, the fact that he didn't know what to expect from Ally bugged him ever so slightly.

"Grandma, they're going to get married right?" Jenny interrupted, thinking this sounded like a bad ending to the story.

"Of course they get married sweetheart."

"They do?" Johnny perked up. "But Ally's some cat thing, how can they get married?"

"Because love prevails over all."

"Are you going to tell us about the wedding?" Jenny asked with sparkles in her eyes.

"Oh no! do you have to?" Johnny scowled.

"No, I won't tell you about the wedding but I can tell you about the honeymoon.

"That's even worse!" Johnny choked. "Why would you do that?"

"Because it was nearly three years from the day of graduation to the day Ally and Jim were married and it was on the honeymoon that Ally changed into a cat again."

"I don't even want to know anymore." Johnny spoke emphatically assuming this was going somewhere that children's ears shouldn't hear. Grandma chuckled at that but decided to explain.

After a few months had passed and Ally hadn't changed into a cat again, Jim just kind of accepted that what he saw that night was just his eyes playing tricks on him. So when he got past that point and was able to focus his attention back on their relationship it began to prosper and grow again. Of course it had taken quite a hit those past few months as even Ally could tell that Jim was oddly distant but she assumed it was cold feet after asking her to marry him. When he finally came back to her, heart open wide, their love flourished like a sunny field on a spring day. While they continued courting and enjoying their prolonged engagement, Cindy had already finished her small part in her first film and was enjoying the attention when she was asked on board another film. This was the reason why she couldn't be at the wedding but she made up for it when she gave them a trip to Hollywood for their honeymoon as their wedding gift.

During their time there they did quite a bit of sight seeing and was even allowed backstage passes to watch Cindy perform and experience how a big-time motion picture was made. It was all quite exciting, but there was a hidden danger that none of them could have been prepared for.

"Cut! That's a wrap." The director spoke into his megaphone. "Bring me the background for scene 176." The hustle and bustle around the lot was absolutely crazy as dozens of people scurried about. "Bring me the background for scene 176." The director spoke into his megaphone again as he stood from his chair and began walking towards the cameraman to make notes.

Ally and Jim had been watching the happenings here for a couple of hours now and it was definitely something they could get into. Ally stood up to stretch and then began to walk around the set while they were at break. She was lost in dreamland thinking about all of the excitement here, about how neat it was that Cindy was going to be in motion pictures, that she knew an actual movie star when something noisy brought her back to reality. A large wooden backdrop being relocated from a different stage broke loose from its rope and pulley system and began to fall in the direction where Ally was currently standing. Ally looked up at this monstrous prop falling towards her and literally froze in fear. Cindy saw the toppling wall falling towards Ally but the only thing she could do was point with her mouth opened wide, not even able to comprehend words at such a drastic and quick time frame. Jim saw this happening and went into quarterback mode running towards her, knowing that he was too far away to help but praying he was wrong.

Unfortunately, as he ran and as everyone watched, many trying to regain the ropes, camera men rolling, purely by accident, Cindy finally screaming, still not able to articulate words. Ally began to react. Spinning around 180 degrees as fast as lightning, she leapt from the spot she was just standing to safety, her dress remaining in that somewhat frozen state until it was slammed down underneath the large wooden background. Jim's eyes peered in on the situation as he watched his wife, a lovely woman, in a blink of an eye leap to safety as a cat, land on all fours and from the explosion of air from the collapsing backdrop, be shoved onto her side where she transformed back as woman, wearing absolutely nothing, naked and stunned into unconsciousness.

Having had basically three years to prepare for this absolutely worse situation, Jim's reaction time was at top speed. He reached over to a costume rack, ripped a robe off of the rack and continued to Ally, sliding on his knees for the touchdown and covering his wife's bare body with the robe. He hesitated none as he arrived by her side and at top speed, he scooped his wife up into his arms and ran out of the production studio as fast as he could. Never looking back, never slowing for a moment, he ran all of the way to the parking lot to their car, placed Ally inside and was just leaping in on the drivers side when Ally awoke. Jamming the keys into the ignition and throwing the car into gear he was peeling rubber out of the parking lot before Ally could ask what was going on.

This was the part he hadn't prepared for. In the months after her first incident he went over everything he could think of in his head regarding this situation. Not how she changed but what he could do to protect her the *next* time she changed. Would he be there for her? Would he be able to get to her fast enough? Would he be able to shield her transformation from others? Would he be able to get her out of there before any questions were asked? Then came the little details. When she changed to a cat the night she fell she remained in her clothes for the most part because gravity pulled them down with her but when she changed back they had gotten torn when her shoulders weren't lined up with the dress's shoulders, the dress had been twisted and the waist was higher, around her chest, it looked as if she had been trying to remove her dress when he pulled her out onto land but since she wasn't breathing and the guy who knew CPR had to rip open the front buttons to get to her chest to begin the compressions, no one else noticed.

But Jim noticed. He hadn't realized he noticed that night but days later while going over every detail of that night for the thousandth time he realized that when she turned into a cat she shrinks and when she shrinks, she runs right out of her clothes. He realized then that the next time, God forbid, this ever happened; he'd have to be thinking about finding something to cover her up as well. If he wouldn't have been in such a panic now, he almost would have been proud of himself, keeping his cool, getting them out of there before anyone had the chance to say something. But right now Ally was asking what happened again for the second time, and that was a question Jim truly didn't know how to answer.

"Jim! Talk to me. What happened? Where is my dress? Why have we left the studio? Why are you driving so fast?"

"Ally just be quiet!"

"Why Jim? What's going on? I don't understand what's going on!" Ally was beginning to cry and this was breaking Jim's heart although his fight or flight responses were still running at full strength. He truly didn't know what he was going to do next. He didn't know how to tell Ally about this. He didn't know how to deal with this. He was now making this up as he drove and as he pulled into the hotel parking lot both of their heads hit the roof of the car when the nose of the car scuffed on the driveway. Slowing very little, Jim continued around to the back of the building, pulled into a spot next to the dumpsters and raced out of the car as fast as he could.

Throwing open the passengers door, he reached inside, grabbed Ally by the wrist and yanked her out of the car with all of his might. Now nearly flying behind Jim, Ally ran with him as he ran in through the backdoor of the hotel, through the kitchen and down the service hallway to the freight elevator. Once on the freight elevator and going up to their floor. Ally again began asking her questions.

"Jim, what's going on?"

He again didn't answer her and when the doors opened he peeked his head out of the elevator, checked to make sure no one was in the hallway, then took Ally by the hand and led her sprinting to their hotel room. Once inside, he closed and locked the door. Ally sat down on the bed and watched as Jim began pacing in the entry way, his hands on top of his head. She was growing increasingly frightened but at this point wasn't prepared to distract him with questions again until he calmed down some. When he walked over to the window, looked outside and then closed the blinds and was walking back over to the door, Ally finally spoke again, calmly and carefully.

"Jim." Her voice was calm and soothing. He stopped but didn't look at her. She waited a moment and then spoke again. "Jim. Can you look at me?" He slowly turned to her and found the face he loved so much. He walked over to the dining table and pulled a chair near the bed and sat down across from her. He straddled the chair, the back of the chair separating them. He hadn't meant for it to be a symbolic play, but he needed to keep some distance between them while he worked through this. He looked at her, those gorgeous green eyes staring back at him with love but confusion. He finally spoke.

"Do you remember what happened?"

"When?"

"Think back. Where were we?"

"The studio."

"Right. What is the last thing you remember?"

"They had just called cut. I had gotten up to stretch my legs…."

"Right. And then what?"

"I uh..." Ally paused as she tried to pull the events into her memory. There was a huge gap. "I was standing... by the stage... and... I don't know."

"Do you remember the backdrop falling?"

"The backdrop... oh yes, kind of, I was under it, right? But I don't remember what happened after that. Did I get hurt?"

"You didn't get hurt. You don't remember what happened next?"

Ally thought about it for a few more moments. "No I don't."

"You don't remember what you did as the backdrop fell towards you?"

"No Jim. Why? What happened?"

"You really don't remember?"

"Jim, tell me. What happened?"

He looked at her stunned for a moment. He knew the next thing to come out of his mouth wasn't going to go over well. Would she even believe him? He just had nothing else to say at the moment. “Ally you turned into a cat.”

“I tripped on a cat? Is it okay?” Ally began with confusion, certain she heard his words wrong.

“No! You turned into a -”

“The cat's not okay? Did I hurt it?”

“Ally there was no cat.”

“But you just said.”

“You were the cat!” Jim yelled angrily too upset to show patience for Ally's confusion.

Ally paused, completely confused. She knew she was misunderstanding him, he was so upset, she was certain he wasn't articulating himself properly.

“Jim, you're not making any sense. Calm down and...”

“”I will not calm down Ally! I'm trying to tell you that you turned into a cat before my very eyes! You were standing there frozen in fear as the backdrop fell towards you, then you jumped clear out of your dress as a small beige domestic house cat and landed feet away from the backdrop and then passed out! You don't remember that?!?”

Ally was truly growing concerned about her husband now. She could not for the life of her understand why he had decided to have a break down all of a sudden. They were on their honeymoon, this was supposed to be a time to celebrate, not join the funny farm. And as that thought occurred to Ally she began to chuckle. Jim was pulling some crazy joke on her. He had to be. “Jim... are we on Candid Camera?”

Jostled, Jim didn't understand Ally's train of thought. “Candid what? Ally, no. This isn't a joke. You really did turn into a cat.”

“Jim.” Ally smiled sweetly at him. “That's ridiculous. People don't just turn into animals.”

“I know that. But you did.”

“Jim are you feeling okay?” Ally leaned forward to place her hand on his forehead. Jim smacked her hand away and then leaned forward and grabbed her by the shoulders.

“Ally, listen to me. You-turned-into-a-cat. I'm not joking. I know this sounds insane but it's the truth.”

By now Ally was getting tired of this joke. Jim was obviously stressed out about something and she was growing tired of the charade. She yanked herself away from Jim's hands and stood up from the bed.

“Jim this is absurd. You're making a fool of yourself.”

“I'm not the one who changed.”

“Actually Jim, you are the one who's changed. If you can't handle being married to me, fine, but don't go trying to place the blame for your inept inability to keep this relationship solid on some lame story about me.”

Jim stood up from his chair now too, his emotions were spread completely across the board and he truly had no idea what words were coming out of his mouth.

"Inept? I'm doing everything I can to keep this relationship sane!"

"What a load of bull! I am watching you literally go insane before my very eyes!"

"I am not insane! I'm telling you the truth!"

"You're a liar!"

"Damn it Ally!" Jim yelled out grabbing her by the arm again but she yanked her arm away from him and backed up a step.

"I want you out of here Jim!"

"Ally just listen to me!"

"Jim I will not have you in my presence while you are acting like this!"

"Ally you have to -"

"I don't have to do anything! I want you to leave!"

"I will not leave, Ally!"

"Jim, I swear – do I need to call the front desk?"

Jim paused. The sudden realization that his marriage was going down the tubes hit him but that came moments after he realized Ally was in no condition to listen to him right now anyways. What he did realize was that he needed proof. As he backed away from Ally with his hands up to show her that he would never hurt her, he dropped his head. "Fine Ally, I'll leave." As he started to walk towards the door Ally was feeling quite emotional. She didn't understand what was happening. She was watching the love of her life walk away from her and she was feeling relieved about it. He unlocked the door, opened it, but before walking out he spoke as calmly as he could.

"Ally I would never do anything to hurt you. I love you." Then he walked out and closed the door behind him. Ally stood there by the bed confused and growing more sad by the moment. Conflicted as to his emotional status Ally knew one thing, that she loved him too. Not quite certain as to why he would make up a story like that or insist upon it or start this fight, Ally knew she didn't want to loose him. However, by the time she came to terms with the situation of her love for him in her head and ran to the door to stop him; when she ran out into the hallway he was gone. She couldn't find him and not knowing where their marriage stood at this moment she began to cry.

"Grandma, Jim's gonna come back, right?" Jenny spoke sadly.

"Serves her right for not listening to him!" Johnny scowled.

Grandma smiled at that. "Time for bed kids."

"Aw!"

Chapter 6

It was nearly a week later the next time Ally saw Jim. She had no idea how to contact him once he left. It was the late sixties after all, they didn't have cell phones back then.

"They didn't?" Johnny perked up. "How could they survive without a cell phone?"

"There was no email either." Grandma added.

"No email?" Jenny spoke in awe, "How did the people back then communicate?"

"We could send letters through the mail or call them from the house phone if they were home or go by their house."

"That's it?" Johnny scowled, "That's like the stone age."

Grandma smiled as she collected herself to continue the story. The grandchildren woke this morning with questions and as they sat at the dining room table eating breakfast they couldn't stop asking questions.

"Stone age or not Johnny, that's how it worked and that's exactly what Jim did.

When Ally got home and Jim wasn't there she

was more sad than ever. She waited two days for him to come back to the hotel room but he didn't. Completely uncertain as to their future she wrote a note to Jim that she was moving back in with her father and left it on the night stand. When she arrived at her fathers house in tears, he knew not to ask about it until she was ready.

What she didn't know, is after their fight that night in the hotel room Jim went to the airport, and instead of flying home he flew to DC. As far as he was concerned only one thing was going to prove his story to Ally and Brad had it.

Over the past few years Joyce and Brad began dating. Their conviction to sit on those pictures and that story had brought them together and their career choice kind of kept them in the same cliques. When Joyce was offered a position as a journalist with the Washington Post she helped Brad get his foot through the door as their professional photographer. To save money they moved in with each other and as their relationship prospered they got engaged.

Jim knew where they lived and knew how to contact them but every time he tried to call them, they weren't home. They put in long daunting hours at the newspaper and although Jim knew they worked there he knew he couldn't just call them at work with this information. When he showed up on their front door step and they weren't home, he waited. It was that evening about eleven at night when they finally drove up.

"Brad there's someone sitting on our front porch." Joyce proclaimed quietly from the passenger side of the car. Brad looked over through the darkness and saw the same figure sitting there. As he put the car in park he left the engine running. "If it looks like there's danger I want you to drive away."

"But Brad..."

"No buts, Joyce, your safety comes first."

As he walked out of the car and closed the door, Joyce shifted her position to behind the steering wheel and waited with uncertainty as he approached the man in the shadows.

"Who are you and what do you want?"

"Brad it's Jim." He spoke as he stepped into the moonlight. It took a few moments for Brad to recognize him but when he did he calmed down and shook the mans hand. When Joyce realized all was safe, she turned off the car and walked up to them.

"Jim? What are you doing here? Where's Ally?"

"Can we go inside and talk?"

"Sure."

As they went inside Joyce offered Jim a drink.

"Whiskey – neat, if you have it."

By now Joyce knew for certain something was wrong and as she brought him a glass she sat down and she and Brad waited to hear what he had to say.

"It happened again."

"What happened?" Joyce asked before thinking.

"Ally. I don't know how to explain it, I don't know how to even comprehend it but it happened and when I told her she didn't believe me."

"Ally turned into a cat again?" Brad chimed

in.

"Yeah man, it was the weirdest thing I'd ever seen."

"Did anyone else see it?"

"I don't know man. I just ran to her as fast as I could, swooped her into my arms and ran out of there. I didn't know what else to do."

"Back up a second Jim," Joyce interrupted. "Start from the beginning. Where were you? What were you two doing? What caused it?"

So Jim told them the story, every detail he could remember. That they were in Hollywood on a movie set watching Cindy. That the backdrop began to fall, that Ally changed then passed out, that he got her out of there and when she awoke she remembered nothing of the incident and that when he tried to tell her what happened they had a horrible fight and he left.

"And you haven't talked to her since?" Brad questioned.

"How can I talk to her? She doesn't believe me. She thinks I'm crazy and man I almost believe her. That's why I'm here."

"What can we do?"

"I need the pictures."

Brad stood up. He had not really forgotten about the pictures but he hadn't thought about them for a long time. He instantly remembered the way he felt the night that Jim first said that to him and became slightly agitated. "Why do you need them?"

"So I can show them to Ally, to show her that this has happened before, to prove to her that I'm not crazy and she truly is a..."

"Freak?" Joyce interjected.

Jim looked at her hurt. "She's not a freak!" He defended his wife.

"Well that's what she's going to think. She's going to think you are still making this story up and that you are trying to make her feel like a freak."

"But I'm not."

"I know that." Joyce stood up. "But at this moment, she needs to hear it from another person. Someone else she trusts." Joyce turned to Brad. "Go get the pictures. Jim and I are going to go see Ally."

The next day when Joyce and Jim arrived at Ally's father's house, Jim could tell that Joyce was nervous. "It'll be okay."

"What if she doesn't believe us? What if she never wants to talk to me again?"

"We're trying to help. That's all we can do."

When Ally's father opened the door and saw Jim standing there with Ally's best friend Joyce he didn't like the thoughts that were going through his mind. He immediately began to wonder if Jim cheated on Ally and that's why she came home. "Is this the reason she's here? The two of you?"

"No sir." Jim spoke quick. "I swear I would never cheat on Ally."

"Then what is this all about?"

"Sir if I may." Joyce spoke quick. "We need to talk to Ally, and I think this may be something you'll want to hear too."

"Ally can you come out here?" Her father spoke loud as he invited Jim and Joyce inside. When

Ally came out of her room and saw Jim standing there she immediately smiled. "Jim!" Then she saw Joyce standing there and she became confused. "What's going on?"

"Can we all sit down?" Jim pointed to the living room. After they sat, Jim began to recall the details of the night Ally fell from the waterfall. He told every gripping detail leading up to the moment she actually fell and he was reaching over the side for her and was watching her fall away from him. Then he stopped. A moment later Joyce picked up the story from Brad's point of view, telling about how he had been taking night shots with his camera and when he heard Ally scream he zoomed in and when he saw the confrontation he began taking pictures. "When Ally fell he followed her down with the camera with his finger pressed firmly on the shutter button. Knowing that the pictures were going to come out blurry at best he couldn't help as a photographer to keep snapping photos." Joyce paused, Jim started back up.

"As I watched you falling away from me my heart was breaking. I was petrified. All I could see was the fear on your face as you reached towards me but fell further away. I wanted so desperately to believe you'd be okay but I could see the rocks below you." Jim paused to collect himself as Ally and her father both waited, nearly on the edge of their seat. Ally's father had heard about the fall but had never heard the details he was hearing now. Ally on the other hand couldn't understand why Jim was telling her about this when what she really wanted to discuss was their marriage and the fight they had in Hollywood but when Jim started speaking again she listened.

"I knew I had to be loosing my mind at that moment because what I saw next I immediately didn't believe. I watched you falling. I put every searing detail to memory because time slowed to a crawl at that moment and as you spun in the air, turning your back to me, I watched in horror as you seemed to disappear from sight and in your place was a cat, falling feet first towards the rocks. That cat landed on all four paws, penetrating the rock like a basketball and bouncing up from it, relanding in the water beside it. The very next moment I saw you on the top of the water, laying face down and quickly sinking. When I saw you, unconscious and drowning I leapt off of that cliff pressing my force to the right in hopes of making it into the deep end and I dove into that water after you. I didn't come back up until I had you in my arms." When Jim stopped speaking, his head down looking into his lap, Joyce picked up the story.

"When he got you to land, and after the CPR got you breathing again, Brad pulled me from the crowd and told me about what he saw. He saw the same exact thing as Jim except he saw it happen through the viewfinder of his camera as he was taking pictures. I went with Brad that night to the journalism department. I watched him carefully develop every picture he had taken that night and when I saw the pictures, even though they were blurry I knew we had all seen the same thing." Jim opened the envelope and pulled the pictures from it. He reached out to hand them to Ally but she refused to accept them. Her father however did take them and began flipping through them. When he came to the ones with the waterfall and seeing Ally falling from the cliff he wanted to cry but he kept flipping through them, slowing as the pictures became more blurry, slowing when he saw the one of Ally half off the page but it was definitely her and then stopping at the next one of the shape of a cat about to land on the rock. He stared at it for the longest time when he breathed the words, "Oh my God." and then finally Ally looked over his arm at the picture herself. She stared at the picture for the longest time, and as her father began to cover his open mouth with his hand, Ally began shaking her head.

"No. This is another trick." She continued to look at the picture, continued shaking her head. "No. I don't believe this."

"We covered it up Ally." Joyce spoke carefully. "We didn't tell you because we didn't know how to. I convinced Brad to keep the pictures hidden, hidden until it happened again." Ally's father looked up at Joyce as Jim began to speak.

"Sir, it happened again. When we were in Hollywood."

"I will not listen to this." Ally stood from the couch. "Not again!" Then she ran into her room. Joyce realized she needed some time to absorb this but Ally's father needed to hear the rest of it.

"Go on son."

So Jim told Ally's father every detail of that

day. How he had planned for it even though he didn't really want to believe it. How it happened, how he got her out of there and then all about the argument in the hotel when he tried to tell her. “Sir she wouldn't listen to me, she refused to believe it and I don't blame her. But it did happen and this is the second time that I know about.” Ally's father sat there with his hand over his mouth, awe-struck. His mind literally couldn't comprehend what he was hearing. It was amazing and unbelievable all at once.

Just then the phone rang and Ally's father got up to answer it. “This is Bob.” He spoke into the phone and listened. “Cindy? Yes she's here.” He listened for a bit longer. “Slow down Cindy, what are you going on about?”

Jim and Joyce exchanged glances and stood and walked towards the kitchen where Bob stood listening. He covered the receiver of the phone with his hand and spoke to Jim, “She’s completely freaking out.”

Jim motioned for Bob to hand him the phone and he listened in as Cindy continued ranting about whatever was upsetting her. “I don't know what the video shows, they weren't even supposed to be filming at the time but they were and when they were splicing the film together and they got to that area and they saw what they saw. Bob it has Ally on it.”

“Cindy it's Jim. What's going on?”

“Jim! Oh thank God! I've been trying to find Ally.”

“She's here. What's going on?”

“Oh thank God she's okay! I can't believe

what I'm seeing but it's all over the news..."

"What's all over the news?" Jim asked while motioning for Joyce to turn on the TV. Joyce ran out into the living room and turned on the TV as Cindy kept explaining to Jim.

"I didn't know what happened to you guys. You both just left so quickly. But the recording, I swear I don't know how they could be making this up. I mean there's no way to fake a recording like this."

"A recording like what?"

"Jim!" Joyce yelled at the top of her lungs once the TV warmed up and began showing the news. Jim jerked his head around the corner from the kitchen to see the TV and when he recognized the production studio backstage and watched all of the commotion of the recording, the people walking in front of the camera, and then his wife, Ally stepping into the frame.

"That's Ally." Bob spoke proud to see his daughter on TV but that pride quickly diminished as the three of them watched what happened next. Jim walked out to the living room, the phone still held up against his ear, the cord unspiraling to it's max length. Cindy was still speaking but Jim was unable to hear her. They all watched as one of the stage hands lost grip of the rope supporting the backdrop. They watched as he scrambled to retrieve it but it slipped through his hands and they watched as Ally, just within the shot of the camera looked up at the wooden backdrop and turned to run and leap off of the visible screen of the recording as a cat. A moment later, the camera man brushed the camera as he ran past it and it bumped right just an inch and showed a cat on it's side that in the very next frame was Ally, laying there in the buff and a moment after that running as fast as he could with a black robe waving in the breeze, Jim ran over to Ally, scooped her up into his arms and ran out of the cameras view.

"That's right folks. Let's show it again in slow motion." The newscaster spoke as the video began to play again.

"Ally! Come out here!" Bob yelled at the top of his lungs. She came out to see the three of them staring at the TV, and when she looked as well she saw what she hadn't ever expected to see. She watched as they played through the video again this time frame by frame, the news person describing every scene in detail. She watched with her own two eyes as she turned into a cat, leapt to safety and changed back, unconscious. She watched as Jim raced into view and grabbed her and she watched as the news person paused the video on one frame, the frame of her in Jim's arms, her head against his chest, her eyes closed, hardly covered at all by a black robe and she could see Jim's facial expression, the look of terror and determination all in one, like he was running the final-win touchdown while carrying the most precious cargo ever imagined. And as Ally looked at this picture, not even able to comprehend what the anchorman was saying, she gasped for breath.

Bob, Joyce and Jim all turned to look at her when she suddenly felt very vulnerable, very much exposed and very naked. She spoke. “This isn't real. This can't be real.”

Joyce walked towards her but she backed away. “Stay away from me!” She yelled as she continued to walk backwards. Just then the anchorman spoke again and put up a new picture, a picture of Ally from her high school year book. “Folks we're not making this up. The name of the woman who turned into a cat is Allison Catsworth and she's from...”

At that moment Ally fainted. Jim ran towards her, the curly wire of the phone yanked at his hand until he released it and the phone rocketed back into the kitchen. Hearing the phone's receiver bang against the side wall and then clatter onto the floor, Cindy continued speaking into the phone. “Jim? Jim?”

Chapter 7

That evening the doctors at the hospital ran a battery of tests on Ally. When she fainted she hit her head on a table and the first thing they had to do was stitch her up and make sure she didn't have a concussion. Jim absolutely refused to leave her side as Bob made his way up the hierarchy at the hospital with various called-in favors from friends to ensure absolute confidentiality of the entire situation. Not sure how far this whole story would go, he had called his neighbors to check in since an ambulance had earlier left their house, only to find that news crews were already camped out on the front lawn waiting to get an exclusive with Allison.

Having heard tabloid trash and seeing how the media treats superstars like the Beetles and the Monkees, Bob immediately went into a defensive mode in trying to determine the best way to protect his daughter. He wanted to be in denial about Ally's ability but with the dangers that were just now brewing, he didn't have the option or opportunity for it. When he said money is no object and the head physicians were relayed on her 'pre-existing condition' a few well placed phone calls brought in a whole super team of specialists. From immunologists, cardiologists and neurologists, to placing calls in for biochemical geneticists and a molecular geneticists who's primary focus is on desoxyribonucleic acid otherwise known as DNA; something that wasn't that well known in the late sixties.

The evening however, was increasingly traumatic for Ally. Even though the doctors explained what they were doing and that they were running tests requested by her father, the tests were invasive and alarming. When they shoved a tube down her throat to retrieve direct air samples from her lungs she choked and gagged, squirming and thrashing around the bed until additional nurses were called in to hold her down. Being confined as well as uncomfortable Ally's fight or flight responses began to kick in. Her adrenaline was pumping, panic set in and as she thrashed, she cried, as she cried she growled and as she growled she began to change into a cat forcing the nurses to release their grips on Ally's arms and legs from sheer fear and reverence.

With a rather large video camera focused towards the table to record every situation, observing doctors and specialists viewed in horror as the fur appeared, the body began to shrink and yet as the aggressors backed away and the assault and tests ceased, so did Ally's amazing transformation. Murmurs about the situation erupted as hypothesis and opinions were embellished, but by the morning they were no closer to answers than they had been when they started.

By the morning Ally was literally surrounded by doctors. Having been through an entire night of being poked and prodded, blood tests, x-rays, she was exhausted and a new team of specialists had just arrived. As they stood around Ally, going over their paperwork, test results and charts and speculating amongst themselves, one man walked in, walked past the group of specialists and directly up to Ally. Sitting there stunned, he shifted his hand out to shake hers and introduced himself.

"My name is Doctor Julius Roberts and I am a molecular geneticist that has been working with other key specialists in the field of DNA research. We have been mapping out the genomes of human, plant and animal chromosomes for years and I feel I may be able to bring a unique insight into this particular situation. With your permission I would like to place my emphasis study upon you and focus my core attention towards deciphering the particular genetics within you that is causing these particular episodes. I will need a sample of your blood now and am hoping to get a sample of your DNA before the first episode happened."

Ally was looking at the man curiously. He seemed genuine enough, and he was actually talking to her, not at her or about her, but what he said he wanted to do sounded scary and she definitely needed more information before she could accept his proposal.

"Excuse me Doctor Roberts, I don't mean to interrupt you but don't you feel since you are coming in mid-stream that you should refer with us before professing your diagnosis?" One of the specialists inquired as the rest of the doctors hushed to hear his response. Dr. Roberts glanced down at the specialists name badge and occupation then looked into the mans eyes.

"It is in my expert opinion that stress tests and EKGs will not get down to the bottom of this predicament. We don't need a cardiologist, there's nothing wrong with her heart, we need to dig down deep within the molecular level of her anatomy to research the reason why her chromosomes are, in laymans terms, mutating under obvious stresses. My in-depth sequence analysis confirms that we are dealing with a mutation of sorts and will need to set our primary focus initially on isolating the gene or genes involved with this mutation before we can even consider devising a cure."

"And what kind of in-depth analysis could you have done since you just arrived moments ago?"

"I've been studying this particular case since 1964."

There were murmurs among the specialists as they discussed the relevance of his suggestions and how he could have been involved in a situation so new so long ago when Ally asked that question.

"Doctor Roberts, how did you know about 1964?"

"Brad Johnson is my nephew and when he posed the question to me three years ago and we began consulting on the possibilities I became intrigued and began my own personal studies not aware until last night that his inquiries were about an actual living person."

"Brad told you about my fall?"

"He told me of a hypothetical situation but didn't provide me the details until last night."

"Do you think you can really help me?"

By now every specialist in the room spoke at the same time. Questions pertaining to the nature of his study, to Allison's past event were all being asked at the same time and when Jim walked back into the room with two coffees in his hand, he spilled one during all of the commotion.

"Ally, what's going on here?" He asked loudly as he made his way to her bedside.

"My name is Doctor Roberts," the man said as he shoved his hand into Jim's free hand. "We should talk."

Over the noise of the other doctors conversations Jim couldn't hear Doctor Roberts introduction. He yanked his hand from the doctors hand and stood next to Ally. He put the coffee down on the side table, pressed his fingers into the sides of his mouth and whistled so loud it echoed in the room. When everyone stopped talking Jim spoke again. "I asked, what's going on in here?"

"Sir, can we talk alone?" Dr. Roberts suggested. Ally took Jim's hand to get his attention and when he looked down at her she was nodding her agreement. Leaving it up to her he spoke. "You heard the man, everybody out!"

Over the next hour, Doctor Roberts once again but in more generic terms explained his field of study, the research he had done on the project thus far and his relationship status to Brad. Although Jim was furious that Brad had gone behind everyone's backs to discuss this he found himself somewhat relieved that they had someone who was already so caught up and ready to get into it.

Dr. Roberts outlined his plan for the two of them and was very convincing until he came back to the part of requesting DNA from before the first incident 3 years ago.

"I'm sorry doc, but how are we going to get you that?"

"DNA can be acquired from blood, saliva, hair, fingernail clippings.."

"Again, doc, how would we get that from three years ago? Ally's not the best house cleaner but I'm pretty sure she's vacuumed up her nail clippings and thrown away her dirty band aids by now.

"Hey!" Ally scolded Jim somewhat playfully.

"Can you not think of anything from three years ago that may have gone untouched?"

"Doctor," Ally pondered. "I think there may be an old clipping of my hair in my baby book. Would that work?"

"That would be more than perfect!"

As Ally's father Bob drove by the front of his house seeing all of the reporters sitting there, he realized he needed a plan B. Driving around the block and parking on the street of the house directly behind his, he made his way through his neighbors backyard, over the fence into his backyard and sneaked in through his backdoor. It was one of the worst feelings he'd ever had, the fact that he needed to sneak into his own home like a common burglar. But he proceeded with his task, going into his late wife's closet, finding the baby box, locating the baby book and retrieving the hair sample.

Satisfied at a job well done, he put the box back up on the shelf, closed the door and walked through the house to the front door, opening it to leave. However once he did that he realized the error he had made as every reporter leapt to their feet and ran towards him with microphones on. Slamming the door and locking it, he panicked for only a moment before anger filled in and he found himself on the phone with the police.

About ten minutes later Bob heard the police sirens approach and one of the cops were on a bullhorn demanding the reporters keep their distance and leave this mans public property. When the two sergeants knocked on the door Bob let them in to discuss the situation and how best to go about privacy and security.

"It seems to us sir that you may need to hire private security."

"Private? Don't my taxes pay you already?"

"Taxes pay us to enforce the laws not be someone's bodyguard. We can assist you this time in getting back to the hospital but you will need to make future arrangements with a private firm."

Two days later Doctor Roberts walked into Ally's hospital room with his results. Bob and Jim were sitting there, Joyce had returned to DC for work.

"Well I have good news and bad news."

"Doctor that isn't anywhere close to being funny." Ally scolded.

"I'm going to do my best to explain the situation as simply as I can. I need you three to listen to me and consider what I'm saying not as speculation but as scientific fact because what I have to say is going to be really hard to swallow. Now I will need to run a gob more tests but initial findings suggest..."

Just then the phone rang and Grandma got up to answer it.

"Grandma you can't stop the story there!" The grandchildren cried.

"I'll just be a minute dears." She laughed as she picked up the phone.

"Oh Lana dear, how are you? How's the ol' ticker?"

As the children waited with bated breath for their grandmother to return they listened as her phone conversation stretched on and on. Growing increasingly impatient they began discussing the story amongst themselves.

"So what do you think the doctor said?" Jenny asked Johnny.

"I don't know."

"I think he's going to say that she'll be fine."

"Fine? Are you kidding me? He just said his news was going to be bad, he's probably going to tell her that she's dying or something." Johnny spoke quick.

"How could turning into a cat kill her? I think she's going to become some hero"

"How do you figure?"

"Spiderman became a hero."

"Spiderman was bit by a radioactive spider, Ally wasn't."

"Well we don't know how she got infected, maybe there was some strange cat bite." Jenny spoke trying to defend her idea.

"We don't know yet that she is infected with anything."

Just then Grandma returned to the kids hearing their conversation.

"Grandma was Ally bit by a radioactive cat?"

"Or was she infected by chemical waste treatment plant?"

"Waste treatment plant?" Grandma questioned curiously.

"Yeah like the Joker on Batman."

"No kids, it was neither. Shall I continue?"

"Yeah, yeah!"

So the next day Bob, Ally and Jim pulled up in front of Bob's house, exhausted from everything that happened at the hospital but relieved to be home.

"Grandma wait! You skipped over what the doctor said!"

"I'll get back to it. Trust me." She smiled.

The three of them had just gotten home, Jim was exhausted. He plopped down onto the couch as Ally excused herself to go take a shower. Bob on the other hand had been lining up appointments to meet with potential security guards. Unsure of anything, not sure if Jim and Ally would stay here or if they would return to their apartment, if Jim could even consider going back to work after all of this media attention, feeling that Ally would never be able to leave the house again, Bob went into protective father mode and was quickly putting together a plan. As he got off the phone he called Jim into his study for a drink and to discuss the situation in-depth.

"We need to start making plans for the near future. I was able to get the police to scare off the media so we could get here but they'll be back. Ally doesn't know this but the reporters were asking everyone in the neighborhood about her. They're putting together their stories and they're waiting for an interview."

"They'll have a long wait."

"We agree, but we can't protect her forever, nor can we be there with her every minute of everyday."

"Bob, I don't understand your rationalization. So there was a few reporters outside the hospital, in a few days time they will have moved on to bigger stories."

"They were camped out here on my lawn Jim! I guarantee they're waiting at your apartment as well."

"I don't see the need for this added security you're talking about."

While the two of them discussed what kind of security if any, they needed, Allison stepped out of the shower, slid on a robe and was combing out her hair when she heard the doorbell ring. The guys were deep in a back and forth discussion so they didn't hear the door bell but Ally did and without a thought about what Bob & Jim were currently discussing she walked over to the door and answered it.

Almost immediately however, she wished she hadn't. Like a barrage of bullets, microphones and cameras were shoved into Ally's face and an array of questions began about her side of the story. Trying to listen to the questions of the media, how can she transform into a cat, had she always been able to do this, does she have any other feline senses, Ally without much thought also began trying to answer.

"I don't know how it happens. I didn't realize I could do it until now."

"So you admit you can do this."

"Yes I suppose." Cameras began flashing, nearly blinding her.

"What do you plan on doing now that your secret is out?"

"What secret? I wasn't trying to..."

"Do you have heightened senses like a cat? Do you have a tail?"

"What?" Ally asked flustered. More questions, crazy questions were being asked, how could she answer them? She didn't know any answers herself.

"Did you hear that?" Bob spoke as he stood from the desk in the den at the back of the house. The sound of the media rolled into the room and immediately he realized something was wrong. Running down the hall and towards the door he watched as one of the young reporters possibly from one of the tabloids reached in and started ruffling through Ally's hair asking if she had cat ears. Flustered and freaked out, Ally swatted the guys hand away from her as Jim slammed the door closed. Ally fell to the floor on her butt, stunned by all that had just happened. Bob arrived merely moments after but heard Ally's question.

"What was that?"

"The media! You can't open the door. You can't go near the windows. You can't offer them any information or give them any opportunity to film you or take your picture! They're vultures!" Bob began berating her. "What were you thinking?"

Stunned, Ally couldn't speak. Jim walked up and kneeled down to check on her.

"Are you okay?"

"God knows what's going to be on the evening news now! What did you say to them?" Bob continued to rant. "What did you do?"

"Bob give her a break! She didn't know!" Jim barked back at the man, standing again.

"We can't take stupid chances. She could have been hurt just now."

"But she wasn't."

"Those tabloids will say anything. They'll drag her name through the dirt."

"You're over reacting."

"Over reacting? Did you see what that piece of crap reporter did to her? Look at her hair!"

"My hair is ruffled but it's fine dad."

"He could have grabbed you, yanked you out

of the house!"

"Well he didn't."

Outside at that same moment, the guy who had harassed Ally was nursing his arm that she had smacked away. As he backed away from the door and the news cameras seemed to focus on him, he moved his hand away from his sore arm to expose what looked like fresh cat scratches, deep and bloody. Cameras snapped pictures and video continued rolling, while many reporters began questioning their camera men if they recorded that episode just now.

As the sounds of the media began to over power the pseudo-serenity of their house, Bob looked out the peep hole of the door and began ranting yet again.

"What did you do to that guy?"

"What guy?"

"Whatever you did just riled them up more! Damn it Ally you have to be smarter than this!"

"Now wait just a second Bob, this was not her fault!"

"Well I don't see anyone else here to blame except maybe you for keeping something like this a secret from me, her own father!"

"That's not fair! How could I have known..."

"Stop it! Stop fighting!" Ally yelled. "Things are hard enough right now without you making me feel worse!"

"I'm not trying to make you feel worse – I'm trying to make you aware of the situation! It's dangerous!"

"That's fine, can you stop yelling now?"

"I'm not yelling!"

"You are yelling!"

"I'm concerned Ally! You're turning into a cat when you're emotional and that's a serious cause for concern!"

"You don't think I'm concerned? My God I'm terrified! I can't even begin to fathom why this is happening to me muchless what Doctor Roberts was talking about earlier! Every time I change it alters my DNA further – he says, I need to keep from changing, well duh! I don't want to change into a cat! I don't want this to keep happening! Do I look like I want this to keep happening?"

Jim took Ally into his arms trying to calm her down but she pushed away from him.

"How can you even hold me? I don't even want to be near me."

"Ally I love you."

"Well that's too bad, isn't it? It's not like you're going to have a normal life with me now, right? I mean what are we going to do, raise kittens?"

"You're being ridiculous."

"You think that's ridiculous? I've been turning into a cat and you think that's ridiculous? I don't want to be an animal! I don't want to be a freak of nature!"

"Ally, you're going to have to calm down." Jim spoke carefully.

"Calm down? How can I calm down? Each time I transform, my DNA changes! That crazy whack-job of a doctor thinks I'm going to transform into a cat and remain a cat forever? How can I possibly remain calm? Tell me Jim how?"

"I don't know Ally, but you're going to need to try."

"Why? Tell me why!"

"Because you're changing right now." Jim said cautiously. Ally spun to look into the mirror on the entry wall and began to panic further.

"Oh my God!" She screamed as she watched her eyes narrow into glowing cat eyes. She watched fur begin to grow on her shrinking face. She looked down at her hands, turning into paws and screamed as loud as she could.

"Ally, look at me. Look at me." Jim pleaded as he braced Ally's face between both of his hands and focused her attention towards him. "Take a deep breath and look at me. I love you. I will love you no matter what happens." Jim could feel Ally's heart racing, her breathing was erratic and the look on her face was still full of panic although she was trying to focus on him. "Look at me Ally. Look into my eyes and see my love. My love for you is true, it will never change..."

"Even if I change?" She began to cry.

"Ally stop it! You are going to be fine. We are going to get through this, you hear me? We are going to get through this!"

"But Jim what if..."

"No. Don't do that. You are going to be fine. Do you hear me? You are going to be fine." Jim could sense that Ally was calming a bit even though he could feel her trembling. Once the physical signs diminished and Ally's face was back to normal, he pointed her gaze towards the mirror and spoke. “Do you see? All you have to do is stay calm and you'll be fine. Look, you're back to normal. See?”

Ally looked at herself, rubbed her hand over her cheek to make sure she didn't feel any fur. “Jim I don't know what to do.”

“Neither do I but we'll get through it together.”

Chapter 8

That evening as Ally slept the words of the doctor kept repeating in her head. She hadn't completely grasped what he was saying earlier that day, not at all knowledgeable about DNA or why it was so important. She remembered his conversation in detail.

"Ally I have mapped your DNA from those strands of baby hair and compared it to the DNA in the blood the doctors took when you arrived as well as the blood they took earlier. I mention all three of those because each time I compared the DNA it was different. The DNA from the baby hair was one hundred percent pure human, the blood sample from when you first got here was drastically different than your baby hair and then the third sample showed slight variances of the DNA before and after. Each sample shows your human DNA but is altered with an additional feline DNA that keeps becoming more pronounced each time you are affected by the change." Ally listened intently as the doctor continued. "The change was minute from the second to the third but it shows that each time you transform into a cat, even when it is just starting but stops before a complete transformation can take place, it alters your DNA each time. Whether a little or a lot, your DNA is getting altered, and each time it changes, the feline DNA looks to be taking over more and more."

"Wait doc. Are you saying that Ally's transformed again since she's been here?"

"That is exactly what I am saying. Two nights ago, while the other specialists were running tests..."

"Wait a second!" Bob demanded. "Are you telling me that it happened again and no one told me? Why the hell wasn't I notified?"

"Sir I am not sure why no one notified you. Unfortunately, it happened before I arrived."

"Then how do you know it happened?"

"I was informed about it after, and then I viewed the video footage."

"Wait – there's video footage too?" Bob stood up angrily. Where is it? I want to see it. I swear if that footage gets out heads will roll!"

"Sir. I need you to calm down. I will put an inquiry into locating the footage for you. But I can assure you that everything that happens in these walls is held strictly confidential."

"It better be."

"Daddy, can you please let the doctor finish?" Ally spoke turning back to the doctor and reminding him where he left off. "You said that each time I change my DNA changes too. What does that mean?"

The doctor looked at the young woman sitting before him and even though he truly didn't want to believe it himself, he reminded himself that science doesn't lie. "There are major differences between human and feline DNA. DNA is what determines what color your eyes are going to be, if you have your mothers hair or your fathers ears. Feline DNA also determines whiskers, agility, excelled hearing, along with the color of the fur and the length of the tail. Your DNA is currently showing majority human female but portions of feline and for the life of me upon examining it I don't know why you aren't showing and feline characteristics or physical properties."

"Well I'm glad she's not." Jim spoke up with a smile.

"Granted, but it leads me down a very different path in my hypothesis for her future. We have seen thus far that every time she changes her DNA changes as well. We can then reason that every time it changes it progressively increases in feline genomes and from there we can conclude that eventually her DNA could become completely feline and when that happens..."

"What doctor? What happens then?"

"We really don't know. Speculatively, my hypothesis would be that she would turn into a cat and remain a cat forever."

As Ally woke that morning to the sound of the phone ringing she was reminded that Jim's latest role as loving husband also now included retrieving fresh blood samples every time Ally changed or began to change into a cat. Taking those blood samples to the hospital last night for study, Ally fell asleep before he returned. As she woke to the sound of the phone then Jim's voice when he answered it, she got up, looking forward to seeing him. When she walked into the kitchen however, he was just hanging up the phone and he didn't look too happy.

"What is it?" Ally insisted. Bob was just walking into the kitchen as well when Jim spoke.

"It's confirmed, your DNA changed yesterday again."

"So I've just got to stay calm. As long as I don't have any extra stress I don't change, if I don't change I don't have to worry about this. Right?"

"Yes and no." Jim spoke as he motioned for Ally to take a seat at the breakfast table. "The doctor wants you to take these findings one step further. He suggested that by possibly determining when this first started or by finding out how this happened it may help him determine how to treat you."

"What do you mean?"

"He wants you to explore the root of the problem. He suggested hypnosis."

"Hypnosis?" Bob questioned aloud. "Isn't that a parlor trick that gets people to cluck like chickens?"

"He suggested a hypnotist he knows, he's very professional and he feels it may help to answer some of the questions we have."

"He really thinks this may help us?" Ally asked.

"It's worth a try."

That morning they contacted Doctor Boris Schlitz and scheduled an appointment for that afternoon. "Doctor Roberts told me you'd be calling. I cleared my entire afternoon for you."

Even though Bob had his reservations in

regards to the actual science involved in hypnosis he watched quietly as Jim and Ally left that afternoon for their appointment. Today he had other plans, he was interviewing security guards. Even though Jim didn't feel a need for it, Bob wasn't willing to take any chances when it came to the safety of his only daughter.

"All right Ally, close your eyes, take a deep breath and relax." The hypnotist began speaking calmly. "Clear your mind of everything and listen only to the sound of my voice." Doctor Schlitz began after explaining what he was going to be doing today.

Ally followed Schlitz's directions, feeling just a little foolish and self-conscious. Trying not to let her biases taint her feelings on the matter, she cleared her mind and prepared to see what was going to happen. Jim was sitting across the room in a chair, watching from afar. The hypnotist had said he needed to sit where Ally couldn't hear him or see him, Ally needed to be alone in her journey. Unwillingly Jim did as he was told even though all he wanted to do was hold her.

"Now Ally, I want you to keep your eyes closed. Relax and take a deep breath and when I say the number five, begin to exhale slowly as I count down. Are you ready?"

"As ready as I'll ever be."

"Okay. Inhale." She did. Ally took a deep long breath and then waited.

"Five... four... three..." Then Ally exhaled slowly. The hypnotist counted backwards from five very slowly and Jim could tell that Ally was quickly going to sleep. A few moments later, the Hypnotist led Ally into her past. "Okay Ally, you are in a dark tunnel, it is the tunnel of your life."

"Okay."

"Do you see a light at the end of the tunnel?"

"Yes."

"Good, walk towards that light. But listen carefully, do not go into the light."

"Okay."

"Now Ally, has the hallway brightened up any?"

"Yes it has."

"Good. Now tell me what you see."

"Well there is a hallway to my left."

"A hallway to your left? Really? It doesn't continue in front of you?"

"Well yes, the hallway does continue straight and there are a bunch of doors on either side of the hallway..."

"Oh good, you found the doors."

"But doctor there are also a bunch of doors along the hallway to my left."

"Really?"

"How many doors are in the hallway to your left?" He waited a moment but then grew concerned when Ally didn't answer right away. "Ally?"

"Fifteen." Ally answered quickly.

"Wow."

"What does that mean?" Jim asked quietly.

"She's had fourteen past lives in this hallway." Hypnotist Schlitz answered in a questioned whisper.

"She said fifteen doors though."

"The fifteenth door is this life currently." Dr. Schlitz replied then continued carefully. "Ally go back to the main hallway and tell me how many doors you see there." He waited even longer than before and then spoke up again. "Ally?"

"I'm still counting. This is a very long hallway."

"Interesting." The doctor paused as he made some notes on his paper. "Okay Ally, go back to that hallway to your left."

"It might take me a minute to get back up there."

"Why? Where are you? I was walking down the hallway counting doors. I had counted thirty two so far."

"Really? How close were you to the light?"

"It was still very far away."

"Interesting." He mumbled as he wrote a few more notes then checked back with Ally. "Where are you now?"

"Just approaching the side hallway."

"Good. How many doors are there again?"

"Fifteen" she spoke after a few moments.

"And are they directly across from each other or adjacent to each other?"

"Adjacent."

"Which one is closest?"

"The one on the left."

"And the next one down?"

"The one on the right."

"Okay step inside the first one on the right."

She opened the door. "I don't understand."

"What do you see?"

"It's last night. Jim's trying to calm me down."

"Doc I don't understand." Jim spoke up. "I thought we were talking about past lives."

"We are. Ally come out of that room. Go to the next door down."

"The one across the hallway?"

"Yes. It would be the second one down on the left hand side."

Ally walked across the hallway and opened the door. "It's the hospital the night they were running all of those horrible tests."

"Interesting. Back out of that room and go to the next one down."

A few moments later, "It's the movie set. Doctor I don't understand."

"I'm beginning to. Keep going back. Keep telling me what you see."

"The waterfall. This is the night that I fell."

"Okay Ally go to the next door."

"But wait! I can see us at the top of the hill. I'm just about to get knocked off of the ledge."

"Ally I need you to leave that room."

"But I want to watch myself change."

"You can't. Ally leave that room now!"

"But doctor I just want to..."

"Allison! You must leave that room before you change because in this life if you watch that life expire you could die today!"

Allison backed out of the room and closed the door but was very scared. "I don't understand." She began to cry.

"Allison when I snap my fingers you are going to wake up. You are going to remember everything you saw here. Are you ready?"

"Yes."

'Snap'

Allison's eyes opened and Jim ran to her. She began to cry and speak all at once. "Doctor I don't understand what happened. Why I couldn't I stay? What are you talking about? How could I die?" Jim held her and encouraged her to breathe and calm down.

"Allison, your situation is unique. More unique than I have ever experienced. I've hypnotized people for past life regression hundreds of times and I have never had any of them have an adjacent hallway with extra doors. None of them have ever gone into a door and saw their current life – it's called past life for a reason. The sheer fact that you saw three of your most current events of this current life in those doors mean something is really different with you and for some reason, those particular situations of yours caused you to create separate doors. Now in my research each door means a past life. It means you died and your soul continued on towards a new adventure; a new life. Now obviously you, Allison, did not die last night when Jim was calming you down, but something happened that caused a door to appear. I have a theory, being informed of your unique situation with recent events but I really need you to go back into that hallway and continue to see what's in the remaining rooms.

"Doctor I want to, but I also want to see what

happened to me. I don't understand why I couldn't stay?”

Dr. Shiltz closed his pen and placed it down on the table in front of him with his note pad. He began to explain his actions as Jim peered closer at his notes. “The reason you never go into the first door is because that is your current life. You can not go into it because it hasn't ended yet. There are theories that the door is locked but even if it wasn't the majority of people believe that if you step into that room you could cause a paradox, a catastrophic chain reaction that could tear your soul from this moment in time to put you back there and that switch could kill you. The theory comes from a case from a very long time ago that someone during hypnosis went into a previous life and stayed too long. They stayed long enough to watch their previous life's self die and in that moment, they too died on the couch. It was a devastating turn of events for the hypnotic community but it lead to an intrigue and new guidelines for all hypnotists to follow. If there is ever doubt or fear that a situation from a past life could cause undesired effects to the patient on the couch; we are to immediately remove them from said danger and wake them immediately for their safety.”

“I understand that, I do, but I don't understand why you considered that moment so life threatening. We all know that I survived that fall.”

“All I do know is that your soul created another door after that incident so there was something about it we should be weary of.”

“She turned into a cat during the fall – do you

think something happened to her soul when that happened?"

"My theory is heading in that direction but I would really like to research her past lives further before I go into it."

"Okay." Allison spoke quickly. "Then I'm ready to go back."

"Before you do," Shiltz spoke as he reached for his notepad. "Can you take a look at this diagram and tell me if it is accurate?"

Allison looked at the drawing and recognized it as her hallway. She took the pen and began elongating the main hallway but stopped realizing it was longer than his paper. Then she focused on the hallway to the left. She counted the 16 doors and saw numbers on them with notes underneath where the doctor had written what she saw. Then she noticed something. "There is something missing," she spoke as she began drawing something on the end of the hallway. "You have this squiggle down here at the end of the main hallway, I assume this is your interpretation of the light?"

"Yes. It is."

Allison duplicated that squiggle at the end of the other hallway. "There is another light at the end of the left hallway as well."

"There is?" The doctor spoke confused and intrigued.

"There is."

Chapter 9

Once Ally had been hypnotized again she returned her attention to the door where she had had that life-altering fall and hesitated as she walked past it.

"Ally please go to the next door down." He waited a moment, "What do you see?"

"Hold on, I'm not there yet."

"Why is there something wrong? Has something changed?"

"No." Ally spoke realizing her curiosity of the fall could be like that old saying – curiosity killed the cat. She focused her attention to the next door down, took a deep breath and then walked in. She watched for a moment and when she didn't speak Shiltz spoke.

"Ally, what are you seeing?"

"There's this gold cat and it's running down the street with a fish in its mouth."

"Are there any humans around?

"No." She spoke and kept watching as the cat slowed to a stop. "Wait, here comes a car."

"Get out of the room now!

Ally ran to the door as she heard the tires screeching and slammed the door closed. "Dr. Shiltz?"

"Ally are you okay?"

"Fine, but..."

"Alright good. We're getting somewhere. Ally stay right there for a moment. Don't go anywhere." The doctor was quickly making notes to his diagram as Jim stood and watched over his shoulder. He wrote the number nine next to the door Ally just saw the cat in, then wrote an eight next to the door across the hall one back, then a seven on the other side, working his way down the hall numerically backwards until he got to the number one with one door left for a zero. He paused. Counting aloud he tapped each door with his pen until mathematically he came to the conclusion he expected them murmured aloud the words "Nine lives."

"What?" Allison spoke still deep in her hypnotic state.

"Allison I want you to walk down the hall to the second door from the end. It should be the very last one on the right hand side leaving one last one on the left hand side." He waited a moment for her to get there. "Are you there?"

"Yes." She spoke, looking at the last door to her right and then across the hall to the last door on the left, then she looked up at the light. It was so bright, and so large and yet it didn't blind her. It was a solid white glow, something she couldn't even begin to explain because something like this in her mind should have been either extremely cold or extremely hot but it was neither. It felt comfortable and welcoming and as she looked into it she felt a pull in her heart to go check it out.

"Alright Allison go through it." The doctor spoke referring to the door on the right.

Allison still looking at the light began to step towards it. As she neared it her senses began to erupt with sensory overload. She smelled something earthy and familiar a sweet harvesty kind of smell that reminded her of some plant from her past but she couldn't remember which one. Then she heard the faint sound of tiny bells jingling and suddenly she seemed to be able to taste the slight aroma of fish...

"Allison what do you see?"

"It's all just white."

"What's white?"

"The light. The light is so white."

"Allison where are you?"

"Walking towards the light."

"Why? Allison stop! Don't walk into the light! Backup." She took a few steps backwards and the light seemed to dim a bit. The dark hallway seemed to illuminate around her and the doors of her past appeared on either side. She turned to the door to her right, remembering why she was here and spoke.

"Sorry. I don't know what came over me. I'm back at the door."

"Are you sure you're okay? Should I bring you out?"

"No, I'm fine. I want to proceed."

"Okay Ally, go through the door." He waited a moment for Ally to do the task, and then he questioned her. "What do you see Ally, describe your surroundings."

"I'm in a laboratory. There are cages of animals, and test tubes and chemicals. It seems very dark in here."

"Look around, do you see a clock or a calendar? Try to find a newspaper or magazine, something that may have a date on it."

"Okay. There is some paperwork on this desk over here." Ally spoke as she walked across the room to the desk and picked up a file folder. "This file says, Project Fe.Trans. I wonder what it stands for?" Ally opened the file and began to read aloud. "Test subject 1046 is experiencing slight trauma due to the nature of the change. He has become solitary and has picked up the habit of licking his hands. He's taking up more of the traits of the average feline rather than the more advanced species we have attempted to mold. Can't move ahead with project Feline Transfer if this doesn't prove successful."

"Ally," the hypnotist interrupted, "dates? Any dates?"

"This entry was written August 22, 1941." The hypnotist wrote down that date. "Was it signed? Do you see a name?"

"No."

"Okay, Ally look around some more, do you see a company name or a name plate on the door? Check the desk maybe even a lab coat."

Ally looked around the room taking in the entire experience. The room was very dark, there wasn't any white light in the room, none from sun light or even lamp light, it seemed to her that it was too dark to be a modern style laboratory like in hospitals. She assumed it was nighttime there and that whoever worked there at the lab had gone home for the day. She looked from the table to a dimly lit portion of the room where many more cages were lined up against the wall. There were animals sitting inside each cage pawing to get out. Ally wanted to help them but with another verbal reminder from the hypnotist reminding Ally where she was, and why she was here she turned her attention elsewhere. She looked over at a bookshelf where a chair was sitting and noticed a white lab coat strewn over the chair, she walked over to the coat, looked at it, then spoke.

"Goldie Givens, laboratory assistant."

"Great.' The hypnotists spoke as he wrote down that name. "Are there any other names around the place? Business name? Owner? Maybe a street name, address? We need information."

Ally looked around the room. There were so many cats in cages, meowing, crying for attention, screaming for freedom, Ally wanted to help them but knew she couldn't. This made her sad to see so many sweet animals in captivity. Obviously being used for some sort of experiments. She wished she could help them. She was deep in thought about this when she heard a loud meow with a growl behind her and as she turned to see, all she saw was a small dog walking around the room. She looked at the dog curiously feeling that the sound she had just heard certainly came from this direction and was most certainly the sound that a cat would make. She looked at the dog closer, carefully, even leaned down ever so slightly to get closer when the dog began to speak. Everything in Ally's being expected to hear a bark but when the dogs' mouth opened and the awkward sound of a cat's meow came from it; Ally completely freaked out.

"A dog just meowed!"

"What do you mean?" The doctor asked.

"A dog just meowed! It opened its mouth to bark and the sound that came out of it's mouth was a cat's meow!" Ally yelled again. "This is freaky! I want out of here!"

"Ally calm down, tell me what else you see in the room?"

The dog meowed again and rubbed its body up against Ally's legs. "Doctor, I want out of here, now!"

"Ally just..."

"Now!"

"Okay, Ally when you hear me snap my fingers open your eyes. Ready?"

"Uh-huh! Uh-huh!"

'Snap'

At that moment all went black and as Ally opened her eyes she found herself back in the hypnotist's office. She sat up from the couch and looked around in a panic.

"That was the craziest thing I've ever seen! Everywhere I go, everything I see has something to do with cats! I must be going nuts!"

Jim leapt from his chair and went to Ally. He wrapped his arms around her, cradling her into his chest and held her tightly.

"Ally calm down." He said quietly and calmly.

"Jim I can't do this is! I know I'm going crazy! I just know it!"

"Ally you are going to have to calm down." Jim insisted with a little more urgency.

"Jim it meowed. The dog didn't bark, it meowed and it rubbed up against me like a cat would."

"I know baby, but you're back now. You're safe."

"Why is this happening to me?" Tears began to stream down her face.

"I don't know, baby. Calm down. Take a deep breath."

"Jim? Why?"

"Come on baby, calm down, you're going to get your fur all ruffled."

Ally looked at the back of her hand and immediately grabbed hold of Jim's shirt, pressing her face into his chest. "Oh God! Don't let it happen. Please, don't let it happen!"

"Ally take some deep breaths, close your eyes, stop thinking about it." Ally tried but she was trembling in fear, terrified that she would turn into a cat and remain the cat. "Shhh, calm down baby." Jim cooed sweetly. Ally was literally trembling in his arms. Her face was pressed so hard against his chest his shirt was getting soaked from her tears. Her hands were clutched around his arms as if she were holding on for dear life. As she listened to his words through the ringing in her ears, she realized it was working but not before the hypnotist stood in amazement, staring at the two of them in awe.

"I heard the stories but I had no idea. I didn't believe it."

"Not now doc." Jim insisted trying desperately to calm Ally before a complete transformation took place. The doctors revelations would have to wait. Someone else freaking out and gawking at her was the last thing she needed. With eyes closed, face pressed into Jim's chest, claws dug into his shoulder, she inhaled his cologne taking long deep breaths. Rocking her back and forth, speaking words of calming, her claws retracted. A few moments later, her tears subsided and he stopped rocking. When she finally felt relaxed enough she pulled her face back and looked at the back of her hand, no fur. As she pulled her hand away from Jim's shoulder he winced and she noticed that she had punctured his shirt; her claws had put holes in his arms.

"Claw marks." She spoke nearly reverting back to a panicked state.

Jim grabbed her hands in his hand and then cupped her chin with his free hand. "Look at me. I'm fine. You're fine. We're all fine."

"I'm sorry." She spoke referring to the holes.

"It's okay, babe."

With jaw dropped and eyes in disbelief Dr. Shiltz realized he had to pull it together and as he looked down at the note pad in his hand he realized he had to stay on topic. Speaking carefully; "We know that one of your past lives have to do with a laboratory and that one of the assistants that worked there was named Goldie Givens. We also know that that particular lab was experimenting on animals, specifically cats and feline DNA so I think we may have determined where this particular issue of yours is stemming from. When you are ready we will go back in and learn more, try to fit these pieces together."

"Not today doc." Ally spoke quietly. "I think I just want to rest."

"Come on sweetheart, I'll take you home." Jim stood and helped Ally to her feet.

"Tomorrow?"

"I don't know." Ally spoke. "Let me think about it."

"But we are so close." He prodded.

As they left Dr. Schlitz was completely bummed. This was the most exciting case he'd ever had, he actually saw with his own two eyes the cat-girl begin to transform. Even though he knew he had doctor-patient confidentiality he couldn't help but want to brag.

Once they were safe in their car Ally spoke to Jim. She had calmed but the dried tears on her face bothered Jim. He hated seeing her sad or hurt and he had a feeling he was in for a world of it with what was going to happen in the near future. As he buckled up his seat belt Ally spoke and what she said caught him completely off guard.

"Jim, I want to go to the library."

"Why?" He asked with astonishment.

"So I can research what I saw."

"What, now?" He asked in shock because all

he wanted to do was go home and relax for a bit.

"Yes." She said with pure determination. "While it's still fresh in my head."

Hours later, scouring through pages and pages of old newspapers scanned in and saved on microfiche Ally came across something.

"I found him!" Ally burst from her chair and bellowed at the top of her lungs. Everyone else in the library stopped their reading and looked up at her like she was crazy. Quickly she realized that it was her outburst that had disrupted the quiet and she apologized in a whisper, then she took her notes and went to find where Jim had been hiding out.

As she walked up to him she noticed he had been reading through old magazine articles on the Fiche system as well. He was deep into reading when Ally walked up.

"<u>$100,000 Reward for information leading to the Finding of Lab Assistant."</u>

"Jim I thought you were going to help me search for the scientist."

"I am. I found an article about the missing Lab assistant Goldie Givens, she had been missing since the night of August 24th 1941."

"So?"

"So don't you remember your hypnotic experience? When you read the journal entry the date was August 23rd 1941 and Goldie Givens is the lab assistant's name you got from the name badge."

"I remember."

"Well you'll love this. Goldie Givens disappeared the night after you read that journal entry."

"Why should I love that? Someone disappeared and was never found?"

"It shows that what you saw actually could have been true."

"I was that close to finding the truth on my first hypnotic experience?"

"You were." Jim said delightfully.

"Maybe we should consider going back, I mean, to find out more."

"Let's see what else we can find out first."

"Okay. So what are you working on now?" Ally asked.

"Trying to find any news coverage that might say who Goldie's boss at the lab was. My guess is he would be the man we're looking for to answer your questions."

"Well search no longer. I found him." Ally said gleefully as she plopped the physicians' magazine down in front of Jim.

"How?"

"You're going to love this, the date is June 1941 and the main issue is about a German Scientist who claimed the evolution of DNA strands could lead to genetically enhanced species of humans."

"Genetically enhanced humans? Why?"

"According to the article, he was trying to make a super-soldier for Hitler."

"What? That's crazy."

"Think about it. Keen hearing, excellent agility, the ability to see in the dark. A soldier like that during World War II, a bunch of soldiers like that, could have been the tipping point the German's needed to win the war."

"Alright, now it's my turn. What does this have to do with Goldie Givens?" Jim asked leaning back in his chair with the look of curiosity on his face.

"It's my DNA that's changing. That dog that meowed at me was obviously genetically engineered with feline DNA. I still don't understand how that pertains to my immediate situation, but it's the strongest lead we have. This scientist claimed he could do it. If by chance Goldie was his assistant, then that ties him directly into one of my past lives."

Jim was impressed. "So what's this scientists name?"

"Dr. Auguste Bizaro. So the next thing we need to do is verify that this scientist worked with Goldie."

"Right. But how do we find him? It says here he was a German scientist."

"Research. We'll have to send out letters to the German government I guess, asking if they've heard of this scientist, asking for a way to find him." Ally volunteered.

"Or the editor of the magazine, maybe someone there will know how to get a hold of him."

"It's a long shot but it's all we've got to go on. Until we hear back I'll continue scouring through these articles in hopes of finding more information here."

"Sounds like a plan. I'll start writing the letters."

"Grandma, why don't they just use the internet. Wouldn't it be faster?" Jenny asked with confusion.

"The internet didn't exist back then."

"Really?" Johnny queried. "No cell phones, no internet, no color pictures… how did anyone accomplish anything?"

Grandma smiled thinking back to those days and how simple they seemed. Compared to the confusion of todays technology; she simply couldn't fathom wrapping her head around it all. While it was neat watching the children find information faster than a lightning strike, she wondered silently how learning from a monitor versus an actual encyclopedia would affect them. Learning wasn't just about the knowledge, it was how you acquired that knowledge, and there was no better way than by flipping through the crisp pages of a soft leather bound book with that memory creating aroma of ink to bookmark it forever in your senses.

"Are you okay Grandma?" Jenny asked noticing she was a millions miles away in her mind. Their Grandma came out of her day dream and smiled. "Of course, sweetheart. Should I continue?"

"Please!"

That evening when they got home they were greeted yet again by a swarm of reporters. Pressing their way through the crowd, Jim slammed the door then leaned against it exhausted. "Do you think they'll give up soon?"

"Not likely." Bob said as he walked in from

his den. “They did a report about the scratch Ally gave that guy yesterday who tasseled her hair. Apparently he decided to go get rabies shots so they finished the report with information on how to verify if an animal is infected.”

“I don't have rabies!”

“Apparently no one told him that.”

“There was also a brief blurb about cat scratch fever but since the guy was feeling okay they didn't embellish upon it.” A tall stout man spoke as he followed Bob out of his den. “Hi I'm George Sintel.”

“Are you a friend of my fathers?” Ally asked feeling immediately overwhelmed by his girth.

“No Ally, I just hired him to be your personal bodyguard.” Bob spoke quick.

“Bodyguard? Daddy I don't need a bodyguard.”

“I beg to differ. If those reporters catch you changing again they'll never leave you alone. You've got to take it easy, only leave the house when you absolutely have to and only if you take George here with you.”

“Bob sir, I happen to agree with Ally. Isn't this overkill? I mean I'm here...” Jim began but was stopped mid sentence.

“Yeah but what happens when you go to work? What happens when Ally wants to go to the grocery store? Until we know these episodes of hers are over and the reporters have moved on we have to take precautions.”

“Episodes? You make it sound like I'm throwing temper tantrums.” Ally griped.

"Well what the hell am I supposed to call it Ally? Your metamorphoses?"

Ally scowled. Jim didn't like it either but her father had a point. Until they knew more it made sense that Ally stay as far away from the lime light as possible. There was no reason to give the reporters anything new to announce.

A few weeks letter Ally received a letter from the magazine. It was an apology letter stating that Auguste Bizarro had passed away about five years ago. Disappointed she kept reading only to find out that he had relocated to the United States after the war but that the magazine didn't know where. The back story, they explained in the letter, was that after his lab assistant disappeared he kind of went crazy and never worked in the field of science again.

"That's great." Jim spoke after hearing Ally read him the letter.

"How's that great? We needed to ask him about his experiments."

"It's great because it confirms he's the scientist we are looking for."

"*Were* looking for." Ally embellished the past tense.

"Granted, but maybe we can ask his family."

"His family? How do you propose to do that? We don't even know if had a family and if he did we definitely don't know where they live."

"We can find out."

"How by looking at every phone book in the country for the last name Bizarro?"

"By finding Auguste's obituary."

"And how will that help us?"

"Think about it, what do obits usually say?"

"I don't know, so-in-so died and the date of his funeral." Ally said throwing out irrelevant information.

"And…" Jim continued picking up where she left off. "He left behind his wife, his children and their names etc. We can look up his surviving family members names and maybe they'll know something helpful."

"Let's hope so." Ally said with a hint of doubt in her voice but hope in her heart.

The task was monumental. The magazine had said he died five years ago September but didn't provide an exact date nor did they include a city or state. Ally and Jim searched through microfiche obituaries from every city for every day in September looking for him. It may have been a daunting task but it was still faster than writing the magazine and waiting another two weeks for a response in hopes they would know the exact date.

Finally Jim came across an obit that looked promising.

"It says his name was August Bizarre, if it is him they misspelled it."

"Not necessarily. When he came through Ellis Island they could have simplified it. What does it say?"

"A New York paper wrote, August Bizarre died in his bed at home. Survived by his daughter Sophia and son-in-law Stephen Laden."

"Alright, now we'll find Stephen and Sophia

Laden and ask them about August. Verify that he was the scientist in the article, verify that he had a lab assistant named Goldie that went missing and see if he has any of his notes pertaining to the experiments he was conducting during World War II. That shouldn't be too hard."

"Yeah right." Ally sighed.

Three days later Ally and Jim were boarding a flight to New York in hopes of finding the relatives of the late Doctor Bizarro. Now that they had the lead they had been looking for, they were progressing forward with their search for answers. They weren't quite sure what they were going to say or do or even what questions to ask if and when they found the family. They didn't want to sound like crazy people, but they knew this was their next step and they would make it up from there.

As Grandma stood to stretch the kids both jumped to their feet. Grandma, where are you going? What about the story?"

"It can wait. I have errands to run."

"Awe." They both hummed but they knew that was that.

Chapter 10

That evening Jenny and Johnny were dressed and ready for bed about an hour before their bedtime. They came downstairs play-yawning and stretching their arms in the air announcing they were ready for bed (*and a bedtime story*). Grandma smiled at that and followed them back upstairs to tuck them in.

As she started to leave, turning out the lights, they both shot up out of bed in unison and began speaking both at once.

"Wait! Where are you going?"

"What about our bedtime story?"

Grandma smiled knowingly. But you both came downstairs looking so tired and an hour before bedtime, I was certain you'd be too tired for a boring old story."

"Oh it's not a boring story!" Jenny chimed up gleefully.

"Yeah, especially if she changes a few more times tonight, like from danger and stuff." Johnny added hopefully.

"Oh, I thought I may have bored you last night with all of that non-internet research they did."

No way!" Jenny began to protest but little Johnny was not one to sugar coat anything except his cereal.

"Well actually it was getting boring but I'm hoping it will pick back up again. It *will* pick back up again won't it?"

Grandma smiled brightly. "Actually, yes it does. In fact the new body guard has his work cut out for him."

"Good!" Johnny chimed up happy.

One week earlier on another side of the country a young scrappy ten year old boy spoke up as he threw down a slightly crumpled Tabloid on the desk "Look at this Stephen." Stephen, his uncle who was always annoyed that his nephew insisted on calling him by his first name took a glance at the paper and then with a sigh in his voice spoke.

"Lady gives birth to thirty pound guppy, so?" He asked as he glanced up at his little nephew with annoyance.

"Not that, here, the top corner." The young man said as he pointed to a girl with half of her face covered as a cat. Stephen read the caption aloud.

"Small town girl turns into cat and back again. Freak of nature or mutant being?"

"What does that remind you of?" Josh asked excitedly.

"My father-in-laws experiment come back to haunt me." Stephen said angrily.

"Grandpas experiment, you thought of that too? I need to find out more!" The young man said excitedly.

"Auguste's assistant disappeared off of the face of the earth almost sixty years ago and he was the main suspect. His life never got back on track after that and he gave up on all of his work. Do you really want to relive that?" Stephen asked with an annoyance and a plea for his nephew, Joshua, to just drop his infatuation on the past and just be a regular ten year old boy.

"He said his formula worked and she changed into a cat and ran off." The young boy corrected.

"And no one found her." Stephen added trying to get his nephew to give up this wasted game of scavenger hunting.

"Right, how could they? Do you know how many stray cats there are in this world, even back then? And even if they had found her, they wouldn't have known it was her, it's not like she could still talk to them human style." Josh insisted.

"Yeah Josh but you're missing the point, this news article is talking about a girl who can turn into a cat, it's a complete load of…" He paused knowing he couldn't cuss in front of his nephew or his wife would kill him. "Just forget about it."

"How can I forget it? This is the closest we've ever gotten to solving this case!" Little Joshua expressed excitedly.

"This isn't one of your Sherlock Holmes detective cases! I mean look at the picture, she looks like that lady who was abducted by aliens in last months issue, they probably just used the same face cropped and edited it a bit and made up a new story. This is a load of hogwash imagined up by someone who gets paid a hell of a lot more money than I ever did to make a quota for a trashy magazine with no morals!" Stephen yelled at the top of his lungs. When he was finished he looked at the tearful eyes of his little nephew and immediately felt bad. "Joshua I'm sorry, I didn't mean to hurt your feelings."

"You're wrong Stephen and I'm going to prove it! I'm going to find her, and solve this puzzle and reinstate Grandpa's good name and reputation and then you'll finally believe me!" He said as he ran out of the room. Stephen leaned back in his chair feeling bad about hurting his nephews feelings but certain that he didn't want little Joshua to get involved.

As Ally and Jim got into their rental car they kept going over their plan, or lack of a plan in their minds. They were about to approach an unsuspecting family, ask them if their grandfather was a mad scientist for Hitler who's lab assistant mysteriously disappeared one night. In hopes of researching his work (*if any still existed*) in an attempt to find out how this may pertain to the situation Allison was going through in hopes of discovering how to fix it.

"Are you sure you want to do this?"

"Do I want to do this? No. But it seems like the next step we should take. There is a reason my past life was about cats and I'm turning into one now. I don't know what it is but we've got to figure it out.

Ding Dong

The doorbell chimed and rang through the small house. Ally and Jim waited at the door for almost a minute before someone walked up.

"Can I help you?" A woman asked as she

opened the door.

"We're looking for Sophia Bizzarro."

"I go by Sophia Laden now."

Ally smiled. "I know you may find this weird, but is there any way we can sit down and talk with you? It's regarding your father Auguste."

Shocked, she paused for a moment. "Please, come in."

After asking if they wanted anything to drink and leading them to the living room, Sophia finally sat down with them, curious as to what this was all about.

"You mentioned you knew my father?"

"Actually Mrs. Laden,"

"Call me Sophia, please."

"Sophia, we didn't know him, we actually have some questions about him."

"Regarding what?"

"His past work."

"Who did you say you were again?"

"My name is Ally and this is my husband Jim."

"I mean who do you work for?"

"We don't work for anyone. We're not reporters. We were just hoping you might be able to help us."

"With what?"

"Sophia, I know that this is going to sound insane but please give us a chance." Ally spoke carefully before filling in Sophia on just about everything leading up to their visit.

"Wow. Well I don't know what I can do. He never spoke about those experiments when I was growing up. In fact when I found an old article about his missing lab assistant and asked him about it he banned me from every inquiring about it again."

Jim looked at Ally with disappointment. Ally was happy that they had found the right scientists daughter but now what? She still didn't know how this scientist fit into her situation or why they were really doing this.

"But my nephew can probably help."

"Your nephew?" Ally perked up curiously and with great hope.

"Joshua, can you come out here?"

Ally and Jim turned to see a young ten year old boy emerge from his room. He had thick reading glasses and an old book in his hand. "Yeah Sophia?"

"I think these nice people here would like to talk to you." As Joshua sat down across from them their curiosity was piqued. When Sophia introduced them however she added on the reason why she was doing this. "My nephew Joshua is unfortunately the foremost expert on anything Auguste Bizzaro." He stumbled upon my late fathers journals after he passed five years ago and since was hooked on the story of his life. I personally don't know how he or any of us can help you with your particular situation but if anyone can figure it out, he probably can."

"Hello Joshua." Jim spoke as he held out his hand to shake his. "This is my wife Ally."

Joshua was staring at Ally rather intently when Ally began to feel oddly uncomfortable.

"Are you her?"

"Her?" She queried the boy.

"The one from the news. The one who can become a cat."

Ally shook her head yes.

"Cool. Somehow I knew we'd meet."

"You did?"

"Your story is so similar to my grandfathers experiments. I mean no one has ever heard of humans turning into cats."

"Well I'm not sure you are much of a comic book reader but there has been a character called Catwoman since the 30s."

"Yeah but that is fiction and it's about a woman who wears a cat costume. Not a woman who's DNA is mutating her into a cat."

"You know about DNA? You seem to be pretty smart."

"I have a high IQ."

"Really? So tell me," Ally began, "What is it about your grandfathers experiments that made you think about me?"

"I probably shouldn't tell you this but I wrote to Dr. Roberts regarding his tests and have read all about his work."

"Dr. Roberts, the DNA expert? Our doctor?" Jim felt almost angry.

"Well he wasn't your doctor at the time. When I got grandpa's journals I was so curious about this DNA splicing that I had to learn more. I discovered Dr. Roberts as the premiere DNA expert and wrote to him regarding his work."

"And he wrote back?"

"He not only wrote back but sent me his notes.

They are way ahead of grandpas time."

"He sent you his notes? Why would he do that?"

"Well uh," Joshua paused, "because I might have portrayed myself as a DNA scientist and offered my services to help."

"And they believed you?"

Sophia was shaking her head ashamed and yet knowingly. "I assure you I did not know about this, but it doesn't surprise me. I wouldn't be surprised if Joshua was doing his own experiments on animals."

"Mom, of course I wouldn't do that. Look at what happened to Goldie."

Ally and Jim perked up. "You know about Goldie?"

"Of course I do. Goldie Givens was grandpas lab assistant. The night she was helping him with a new serum of feline DNA the lab dog went berserk and started this huge commotion in the lab. The syringe of formula went flying through the air and stabbed Goldie in the neck and moments after she pulled it out grandpa watched her turn into a cat. As soon as she did the dog began to chase her and she ran right through the window. Grandpa couldn't stop her."

"Holy cow," Jim spoke as he stared at Ally. "The meowing dog."

"What happened next Joshua?"

"According to grandpas journal he ran out to find her screaming to anyone nearby that they needed to help him find his lab assistant she was a small gold furry cat and he was eventually taken into a psychiatric ward."

"They took him to a psych-ward?"

"Well yeah, who ever heard of someone turning into a cat?" Ally and Jim exchanged glances. "Well I don't know the exact details of the timeline for the rest of this because grandpa couldn't write in his journals while they had him, but eventually the police realized that Goldie Givens was a real human and she had gone missing and there was this huge search for her and a reward and when she was never found they assumed grandpa killed her and hid the body but there was never any evidence to convict so when he was finally released from the psychiatric ward he decided to move to America for a fresh start."

Sophia brought in a fresh pitcher of tea as Ally and Jim sat back on the couch.

"Okay, so where does that leave us?" Ally asked aloud trying to figure out their next move.

Joshua perked up. "Well I really didn't know how you fit in to all of this until this morning."

"How do you mean?" Ally asked curiously.

"The article in the paper."

"Which one? The one about the reporters cat scratch?" Jim asked certain that was the latest article.

"Oh no, that's old news." Joshua spoke, "You don't know do you?"

"Know what Joshua?" Jim demanded.

Joshua stood and went to his room. Jim watched him leave then looked at Ally. She shrugged her shoulders. When Joshua returned he handed Jim a cut out newspaper clipping. "It's from today's paper."

Ally leaned over to read the headline with Jim, 'Ally Cat's 9 Lives' Hypnotists tells all about Allison Catsworth's past life experiences.

"What the hell?!?" Jim stood from his chair angrily. "Do you have a phone?" Sophia nodded her head and led him to the kitchen as Ally reached for the paper but Jim took it with him. She looked over at Joshua begging to know more.

"It tells about how your current life seems to be going through a cats life cycle, you know, nine lives and how that explains the new doors each time you transform and then he goes into the scientists lab and the feline DNA research. It seems his theory somehow combines past lives and human souls and I don't really think he's completely figured out how this is working but apparently he felt he knew enough to break patient doctor confidentiality clauses so he can get his name on the front page of every paper across the country."

Just then Ally heard Jim yelling in the other room, she and Joshua both got up to go listen.

"What do you mean there's nothing you can do? This is an illegal invasion of privacy! Well we'll just have to see what our lawyers have to say about it." Jim yelled and then slammed the phone onto the receiver. He then picked up the phone and made another call. While it was ringing, Ally tried to find out what was going on.

"Jim, who was that, what's going on?"

"It's us. Yeah we just read it." Jim listened to the other person on the line for a moment as Ally again tried to inquire as to what was going on. Jim put a finger up to ask for a moment then spoke again. “I understand. Yeah we're fine.” Ally waited intently as Jim continued having this back and forth conversation with someone but she had no idea who and not knowing was driving her crazy. “Really? Yeah put him on. Dr. Roberts, yes we read the article.” Knowing that Jim was on the phone with Dr. Roberts helped to ease Ally's curiosity but not knowing what he was saying began to get to her again. “The guys a quack. But what he did was unprofessional.... You don't need to apologize for him. Go ahead.” Ally raised her eyebrows, did the physical body language for 'come on tell me what's going on' when Jim once again raised his finger to give him a moment. Ally threw up her arms and stormed out of the room. Jim then made the sign for he needed a pen and paper and Joshua quickly handed Jim their on-going grocery list. Jim flipped it over and jotted down some information he was being given. “Got it. Thanks Doc. Yeah, we'll be careful.”

As Jim hung up the phone Ally ran back in the room, not having gone far and immediately began her inquiry.

“Well, what was that all about?”

“The newspaper won't retract the article. Your father is fine although he’s grateful he installed that security system and furious we don’t have Mr. Sentinel with us and Dr. Roberts made a house call to personally apologize for referring us to that quack hypnotist.”

“Is that all?”

"No." Jim stopped and motioned for the two of them to talk secretly. Sophia took Joshua by the shoulder and led him out of the room as Jim showed Ally the paper he just took notes on.

"We need eggs and milk?"

"No." He grumbled as he turned it over. "We're to go here and get a case of syringes and vails. Dr. Roberts is now somewhat convinced that the hypnotist may have been on to something and he wants me to take blood samples of you every time you change and send them to him so he can keep track of your progress as we travel."

"What does he think is happening?"

"If he were me," Joshua ran in interrupting them, "he'd be thinking that grandpa's formula is still somehow in your system and continuing to work and mutate."

"But Joshua, that doesn't make any sense. I am not Goldie Givens, I'm Allison Catsworth. I was never injected with his formula."

"True, but you are Goldie's after life."

"Grandma, who were we before?" Jenny asked obviously caught in her own inner story.

"What do you mean sweetheart?"

"My past life, who was I?"

"Sweetheart, I don't know if you have a past life and even if you do, I have no idea who you may have been." Her Grandma answered honestly.

"We should go see a hypnotist tomorrow." Johnny spoke up, "Maybe I was some soldier and I died on a battlefield."

"Grandma do you think I was a princess?"

"Sweetheart, I don't know what you were, but I know you are my princess right now.

Johnny was now standing on his bed pretending with his arms that he was shooting a machine gun as a soldier, and then play acting that he was shot and fell down onto his bed with a bounce.

Grandma stood, and tucked Johnny back into bed, "I guess it's bedtime."

"Already? But it was just getting good. I like the kid." I did too. Grandma admitted. As Jenny said the same. Grandma sat back down on Jenny's bed, "Are you sure you want me to continue?"

"Yes!"

Before they left, Ally and Jim discovered that Joshua had already begun a search for his late grandfathers scientific research. He had read in Bizzare's journals that he kept extensive records of all of his work but that it had all been confiscated after Goldie's disappearance. He had written back and forth to Germany many times trying to locate more information and through these communications found that there was a great possibility that much of his research had been transported overseas and was currently stored in the National Archives. "Unfortunately you need to go there in person and you also needed to be of a particular age to get in" Joshua admitted bitterly, "so up until now, I didn't think there was anything more I could do."

Jim was intrigued, especially when Joshua mentioned that his grandfather might have made reference to a reversal. Joshua insisted that Jim take his grandfather's journals with them.

"I couldn't take these. They're all you have left of him."

"Well I'd hope you'd give them back when this is over but I really think you'll need them. They refer to specific files and experiments sometimes and if you do go to the archives you may find they'll come in handy."

"Thank you Joshua."

"No, thank you. I can't do it myself so I need you."

They exchanged phone numbers and Ally and Jim left with a stack of old journals, knowing well what they meant to Joshua. Jim also knew that the possibility of needing to make a trip to Washington DC was inevitable, but as of right now he couldn't fathom leaving Ally's side.

Chapter 11

Ally's father Bob was sitting in the bank discussing finances when he was turned down once again. He had decided to plead, to get down on his knees and beg but when the bank again declined his loan he understood. How could they truly loan a man this much money when they knew that he could never pay them back. As he sulked out of the bank he was at his wits end. Ally's doctor had been so kind. He had gone pro bono on all of his services. Everything he did for them, every hour he spent was free, he was doing this to learn.

However every test he took, every x-ray and blood test cost the Catsworth's and the hospital was not willing to give all of that away for free. When the reporters became an issue Bob hired protection, he had to because the police force couldn't help, but that protection cost too. The traveling, the hypnotist, the rental cars, not to mention the extra mouths to feed on a retired mans income, his savings was quickly spent and Jim couldn't get a job and help with everything he was doing for Ally. Even if Jim wanted to get a job, the reporters would hound him until he lost it. The bills were already piling up, the stress was overwhelming and the bank had rejected his pleas. Bob was at his wits end when Sandra Pike bumped into him on the street.

"Mr. Catsworth, how are you doing?"

"Do I know you?"

"Sandra Pike, Prairie Dust Tribune."

"Oh I'm sorry. I'm not up for any interviews right now."

"I don't mean to bother you but is there something wrong?" Sandra asked.

"I know it's just the reporter in you but please, just leave me alone." As Bob walked away Sandra grew ever more curious. She decided there was a story there so she walked into the bank and began nosing around.

Jim and Ally drove to the local hospital the next day per Doctor Roberts instructions to overnight a vail of blood to him. Then they traveled to a nearby town to settle down for the night. Everything had been relatively quiet since they left Joshua's. They had checked into the hotel room without any problem so they decided to play on their luck a little bit more and take advantage of a beautiful night in a beautiful town.

It had seemed like forever since they spent any real time together. Sure they had been inseparable since this thing started but to Jim, it seemed more like a job rather than a marriage. He loved Ally and knew that even though they were going through something really difficult, he also knew that they couldn't stop living their lives. With some encouragement, Jim convinced Ally to go out for dinner.

They were enjoying themselves completely when someone recognized Ally. But he didn't approach her. He wanted to be the person who informed the media where she was. He knew he would get mentioned in the article when they arrived if he knew anything about them. So he walked to a pay phone across the street and started making phone calls. Before he knew it media vans were pulling up in front of the restaurant and he was making his way up front to meet them.

As the crowd of reporters ran up to Ally, Jim stood up. "Ally, we've got company!" Ally turned to see the cameras and lights and microphones and people all racing towards her and her heart skipped a beat. She stood right as the crowd surrounded her. The questions were all asked at once making it sound like a deafening roar. Ally tried to shield her eyes from the flashing lights and was quickly growing terrifyingly scared. Jim tried to protect her but he too didn't know what to do. Before either one of them knew what to do next, reporters began fighting over her, pulling her apart limb by limb. Ally was screaming, she didn't know where to go, what to say or what to do. And as she began to panic, feeling vulnerable and scared, her emotions were too high and she began to change.

"Finally!" Johnny exclaimed as he leapt from his pillow.

"Johnny hush! I want to hear what happened!" Jenny scolded him.

Jim saw it happening and although he tried to hide it from the reporters he knew it was going to happen and he also knew there was nothing he could do. Within moments after the attack, Ally had turned from a frightened young woman into a tiny gold cat racing between the reporters feet and towards the door. However the door was closed and as a cat she wasn't big enough to open it. She skid to a stop and turned to see the reporters turning their attention to her again.

"Where did she go?"

"She changed into a cat!"

"Did anyone get that on film? Three news crews said yes.

"There she is!"

"Get those camera's rolling!"

"Don't let her get away!"

Jim had just pushed his way through the crowd and was running towards the golden furred cat but so did the rest of the reporters. Jim had no idea what Ally was thinking, there was no way of communicating with her and he had no idea if she would even understand him if he said anything to her. But before he could make his way to the frizzed tailed hissing feline someone opened the door and as they walked in and the cat ran out.

The camera crews stayed focused as the cat ran down the sidewalk until it had disappeared completely then they turned the cameras to Jim who was standing there in shock. Ally was gone and he had no idea where she was going, if she'd be safe or where he could find her. As the cameras and microphones were shoved into his face he became speechless.

"Who are you?"

"Do you know where she went?"

"Can she understand people when she is a cat?"

Jim threw a ten-dollar bill at the first waiter he saw to pay their tab, then he too ran out of the door as quickly as he possibly could. Although the camera crews and reporters tried to follow him, he out ran them, they just couldn't keep up with them lugging all of their equipment and gear. Jim ran down the sidewalk and began calling Ally's name. He made his way completely around the block before he realized he was looking for a needle in a haystack. As he made it back to his car he decided the search would be quicker and easier if he could drive. He didn't know where to look but he knew without fail, that when she turned back again, she would be without clothing and he would need to be the first to find her.

Hours later Jim was beside himself with grief. He had absolutely no idea what happened to Ally or where she was and he literally didn't know what to do next. Feeling completely helpless, he finally returned back to the hotel and prepared himself to call her father. As he parked the car and got out he heard rustling in the bushes across the way. He looked around, expecting to see reporters although he didn't know why, when someone emerged from the bushes and ran towards him. Startled at first, preparing to fight back, his spirits soared when he recognized it was Ally.

Wrapping her up into his arms he kissed her and held her like he should have that first night, when he realized she was standing there in a construction tarp. Quickly he led her around to the back of the hotel and sneaked her up to their room. Once inside, Ally's first instinct was to shower as Jim stood in the closet looking for clothes for her to wear.

Standing there, looking at her dresses, Jim grew upset with tonight’s happenings. He completely didn’t like the idea of all of those reporters hounding them, he didn’t like the idea that Ally got so scared that she changed into a cat and ran off. He didn’t like the fact that now these reporters now had video tape of that happening or the fact that they now had her clothes that she left behind. He didn’t like the idea that when Ally changes back she’s completely naked and helpless and he didn’t like the idea that she doesn’t know or remember anything when she’s a cat.

“Tonight was unacceptable.”

Ally finished rinsing her hair then reached for a towel. “What do you mean?”

“We can't have a nice dinner out without reporters showing up. How on earth did they find us?”

"Someone must have recognized me." Ally said as she wrapped herself in a bathrobe and came out from the bathroom.

"When you ran as a cat, I tried to run for you. I wanted to help you but you ran from me."

"I did?"

"Don't you remember?"

"No."

"I don't understand. What don't you remember?" He continued.

"Jim I don't remember anything! All I know is one moment I was in the restaurant and the next I was laying behind a dumpster naked. It is the most unnerving feeling I've ever experienced. Then when I couldn't find you and I didn't know where you went..." Jim pulled her into his arms as she began to cry.

Later that evening after Ally had gone to sleep Jim found himself still wide awake and pensive. He was in the process of preparing another vail of Ally's blood for the doctor when he finally sat down to relax. He began to think back to tonight, all of his worries and fears for her. He loved her so much and to see her going through this was killing him. He didn't know how to handle it. He knew his fears and insecurities weren't helping matters but he couldn't help it. He was scared too.

The night he saw her falling scared him to death, the idea of loosing Ally was enough to kill him on the spot but to see her change in front of his eyes, to see her save herself changed something in him. His love for her was strong, and he loved her even more now, but he began to worry that his love wasn't as much love as it was pity. He knew what she was going through. He knew she was having just as hard a time with this as he was but he didn't know how she felt about *him* anymore.

Ever since Hollywood things had changed. They tried to get back to their regular life but the people wouldn't let them. After Doctor Roberts started working with them, they had little to no time for anything else. They got involved in the hypnosis then began researching Ally's past lives and here they were. Sitting in a hotel room in a different state worried about the reporters finding them because of the hypnotists' big mouth. Now the entire tabloid reading world knew about Ally and tomorrow morning every news watching American would too.

Jim recalled tonight's events and then their discussion afterward as he sat at the table looking at the vail of blood in front of him.

"Ally I know this isn't your fault and I'm not angry at you."

"Could have fooled me."

"I'm just angry in general. I don't want people to see you on the street and say there's the cat girl. I don't want them to chase you down or touch you or record you. Those reporters frightened you enough to make you change! Do you know how much that upsets me?"

"I know, but…"

"Ally, we don't know what's going on here. We don't know why this is happening to you. All we have is speculation, rumor and curiosity and one really scary theory that says each time you change you loose a feline life, and we don't know what really happens when your lives are lived up. Do you have any idea how much that scares me? You may already be out five lives! And now with what the reporters recorded tonight, it'll be out on every television station and magazine by morning. Everyone in the country will know your face! What's going to happen then when they begin to hound you, to find out more and you get scared, change and run off again? You can only do that four more times before your nine lives are up and then what? You die? Turn into a cat forever? I can't handle that Ally!"

Ally got up and went to Jim, she pulled him into her arms and hugged him for a moment. Then when he was a little more calm she spoke in a very soothing whisper.

"We don't know if that story is true. Nine lives could be just an old wives tale that means nothing to what's happening with me. You don't know. Doctor Roberts will figure this thing out before anything bad happens to me. You'll see. Everything will be just fine."

"I hope you're right." Jim said sadly as he kissed Ally on the lips.

Chapter 12

That night while Ally slept Jim read through Dr. Bizzare's journals. They were quite interesting but many times during the reading they referred back to a particular book or a separate journal that Jim didn't have and he knew then that Joshua was right. There was more that needed to be learned.

The next morning Ally and Jim caught a plane back home. The trip was relaxing however Ally and Jim didn't talk. Ally couldn't quite figure out what was on Jim's mind but instead of just coming out and asking she kept quiet, waiting patiently for Jim to tell her when he was ready. She worried that whatever was on his mind wasn't good and she feared any bad news right now would just push them further apart from each other. They were just exiting off the plane when Ally's father Bob ran up to them. Shocked at his urgency they paused where they stood.

"Hurry, before they find you!"

"Dad! What's going on?"

"Reporters are on their way! We must hurry!"

"Reporters? Why? How did they find out?"

"They must have called the airlines, we've arranged for a backdoor exit, quick this way."

They raced down towards the back of the hallway that led up a flight of stairs to the parking garage. There Bob's car was waiting, a driver in the front seat, the engine was revved up and ready to go. Bob rushed the both of them into the backseat, threw them a blanket to cover up with and then hopped into the front passenger side giving the order to drive. As the car swerved around the corners of the garage and pulled out onto the road, Ally and Jim noticed a stampede of reporters rushing their way, everyone was running down the street to catch up to the car but the driver sped away. Before long the crowd of reporters were just specks in the back window. They had gotten away safely.

"Dad what was that all about?"

"I'd like to say it was the newspaper article but…" He paused looking over at the driver. "Ally you haven't met Samuel yet have you? I just hired him."

"Why did you feel the need to hire a driver dad?"

"Well, he's not just a driver, but I figured we'd need the help. Especially from someone with expert driving skills to get us out of any situation."

"A bodyguard? A driver? Dad am I missing something?"

"I'm afraid so, but lets just say you'll be glad they're around soon and leave it at that."

"Dad, I don't need a bodyguard or a driver."

"I think you do." He protested.

Just then Bob's previous words repeated in Jim's head and he grew curious about them. "Bob, what did you mean when you said you'd like to say it was the article?" Bob hesitated for another moment, by now Ally could tell her father was hiding something.

"What is it daddy?"

"Well, this reporter… she heard something... and the town... this is hard to explain…"

"Daddy?" Ally asked wearily.

"You'll find out soon enough. I think it best you hear it from them."

"Who? What?"

"You'll see."

As they came around the corner to their street Ally saw a large gathering of people and again she feared the worst.

"Daddy – all those people."

"It's okay Ally. Trust me."

As the car drove towards the house and up the driveway, the crowd of people parted. Bewildered, Ally and Jim stepped out of the car and was greeted by friends and neighbors, colleagues and strangers. Everyone wanted to shake their hand and wish them luck. Ally appreciated the kind words but was still confused when Sandra Pike walked up and personally introduced herself.

"I've heard a lot about you. I've talked to a lot of your friends and neighbors and everyone had such wonderful things to say about you."

"Who are you again?"

"Sandra Pike with the Prairie Dust Tribune."

"So you've been asking about me? For what? Some article?"

"Yes and no. I don't want to portray you as some freak like the tabloids have done, my goal was to get your story, to put a real human face and history to this ordeal a human interest story so the rest of the world could get to know the real Ally Cat."

"Okay?" Ally questioned.

Jim was listening and somewhat agreeing but also feeling overprotective in his desire that no one else needed to know. "Well what if we don't want any more stories done about her? What if we just want to be left alone?"

"I can understand that and sympathize, really. But the reality of your situation is the story is out there. The change has been caught on tape numerous times. Everyone in the country knows about you now and the only story that is really going around as of yet is look at the freak of nature and that I feel is unfair to you."

"Right?" Ally was still with her but awaiting the catch.

"Joyce was very helpful regarding the back story. Brad although hesitant showed me the picture but it was good to know that it was a life saving transformation. When I bumped into your father and he wouldn't talk to me I realized the story was more in-depth which is why I went in to talk to the banker and although he didn't want to tell me the whole situation I was able to decipher that between the medical bills, bodyguard and traveling that times were getting tough for you all..."

Ally peered back at her father quizzically but Sandra continued. "When the hate mail began pouring in and death threats, your father found himself a little more eager to talk, especially after I had been able to start a fund for you."

"Death threats?" Jim questioned of Bob, angrily.

"It's stupid stuff and the police are looking into it." Bob began to explain but Sandra continued.

"The town really thinks the world of you. And they feel that even though what is happening to you is completely unheard of and no one really knows what to think about it, they realize that you are a good person who doesn't deserve the bad publicity and when they heard about your financial problems they all decided to pitch in and help."

"Dad what financial problems? You never said a word about..."

"Allison," Sandra interrupted again, "A parents job is to protect his child. It's not your fault of course but that responsibility has grown and unfortunately after last night, it's about to become harder. The town wanted you and your family to be able to focus on your situation, getting better, without having the stress of finances holding you down. Which is why we want to present you and your family with this check of one hundred and twenty four thousand dollars."

Ally looked at the check and then at Jim then up to her father. Tears were collecting in her eyes and although she still didn't know all of the details, she realized things had tried to get hard and it was her friends in this town that were trying to make them better. Disoriented but appreciative she looked out at the crowd and smiled. "Thank you" The crowd of people, friends and neighbors all cheered and Ally felt herself flush with emotion. It was a good feeling though and she wasn't afraid about turning into a cat.

"Awesome." What great friends Jenny cooed romantically.

"A hundred thousand dollars? That would buy like a jillion video games!" Johnny added.

"So things are going to be okay now?" Jenny asked.

"Actually there is still quite a bit to go. Four more lives in fact."

"Oh! Does she die? The nine lives thing is gonna happen?" Johnny asked with shock.

"I can't tell you until I get there in the story."

"Then can you keep telling the story Grandma?"

"Yeah, please?"

That evening Ally was unpacking their bags when Jim sat down on the bed with a very deep sigh. "Quite a day huh?"

"Quite."

"You have a lot of friends here, supporters, family and now a bodyguard and a driver…"

"Yeah, and you." She added happily.

Jim smiled back at her then it faded. Seeing this Ally began to feel uneasy as Jim took a deep breath and spoke again. "About that... I think we need to talk." Jim said glumly.

Oh God, Ally thought to herself in a panic. This was it. Jim was going to tell her he needed to move on without her. Jim had finally decided that he had had enough and that he wanted to have a regular life and was going to leave her. Her worst fear was about to come true and she knew it by the look on his face. Her heart began to beat harder in her chest as the fear grew and not knowing how else to express her sadness, Ally began to cry.

She knew she couldn't deal with this now, especially with all of the added coverage on her. She was already stressed out and if Jim left her now, because he couldn't deal with it, she'd likely kill herself. She needed him more than he knew and she was prepared to tell him so no matter how pathetic it might sound.

"Jim don't leave me!"

"Ally I have to. It's the only way." Feeling that Ally must have already knew that he was planning the trip to Washington DC for research he was somewhat befuddled about tears but assumed she was just afraid of being alone. With that in mind he reminded her of all of her friends and family here and insisted that she would be safe.

"Jim you don't have to leave, we'll figure this thing out together."

"Ally as much as I want to, you know I can't."

"I don't know that! We can figure this thing out together."

"Ally it's too dangerous. You can't be out there anymore and I can't do what I need to do here."

"But Jim, after all we've been through together…"

"Yes we've been through a lot, but you can't go where I'm going."

"I don't understand. You always said we can get through anything as long as we're together."

"Ally I don't understand you. I thought you would agree. I thought you would encourage me to go."

"Why would I do that?"

"Because you know that I won't be able to get what I need if I'm always being hounded by reporters. I need to be left alone."

Ally began crying more, she stood up to begin pacing but Jim could tell she was about to loose it.

"Jim how could you do this to me? I thought you loved me! I thought you wanted to be with me forever!"

"Ally I do love you, but you know I have to do this." Jim continued trying to explain things although he knew they were going bad and he couldn't figure out why.

"When did you decide this? Why didn't you talk to me about it? We could have figured something out. We could have talked about it."

"Ally there's nothing to talk about. I have to go and you have to stay. As much as I'd love for you to go with me, you can't. Don't you see?"

"All I see is a scared man who's running away!" Ally yelled at him angrily.

"Running away? I'm trying to help you!" Jim yelled back.

"By leaving me?"

"The National Archives won't send the files here. I have to go there."

"National Archives?" Ally calmed, wiping her cheeks with the back of her hand.

"Yeah?" Jim said questioningly wondering what Ally had been talking about.

"You mean you don't want a divorce?"

"A divorce? Ally is that what you thought?" He questioned with a laugh.

"Jim it's not funny!"

"Ally I love you! I want to spend the rest of my life with you and I want to do whatever it takes to make sure that it's a long, peaceful life."

"You do?" Ally asked confirming.

"Of course baby."

"Oh Jim, I love you." Ally exclaimed as she walked up to him and hugged him.

"Yeah!" Jenny shot up from bed with excitement. "I knew they were going to live happily ever after."

"That's not the end is it?" Johnny asked with a large amount of disappointment.

"Of course that's not the end." Grandma admitted, "but I think it is for tonight."

"Awe, Grandma! Can't you tell us a little bit more?"

"No, I don't think so. I think this is a very good place to stop for the night."

"But what about the mutant changing and the death-defying stuff, you promised!"

"I said it was coming up, and it is, but I think we should finish it tomorrow."

"Okay, but like tomorrow morning right?" Jenny asked wanting to make sure they got right back on to it.

"Actually, I have a doctors appointment tomorrow, so it will have to wait until the afternoon at least."

"Oh." Jenny spoke sadly.

"Grandma are you okay?" Little Johnny asked, inquiring about the doctors appointment.

"Oh yes dear, just a little blood work. Nothing to worry about."

"So tomorrow after lunch, right?" Jenny asked to confirm.

"Sure, sweetheart. Tomorrow after lunch."

"Good!" Jenny smiled as she laid her head on the pillow.

Grandma knew she had them hooked. She kissed each on the forehead and walked to the door and turned off the light. As she looked back at the children sleeping she knew this was a deep story for them but they are the same age as Joshua was and they are just as smart. She knew it would be okay.

The week flew by and before anyone knew it, Jim was off to catch a plane with an open-ended plane ticket. He was off to Washington DC for an extended trip and as he kissed Ally goodbye, there was a huge part of him that just wanted to stay.

Ally knew that Jim wouldn't give up on his search or his love and that she would see him again really soon. She prayed he would have luck in a speedy find and a quick return but she knew he may be gone for a long time. As she kissed him goodbye that day at the airport terminal a lone tear streaked down his cheek. Jim kissed her one last time then took her face into his hands. Focusing her attention towards his eyes and then he spoke in his signature deep loving voice.

"No matter what happens, remember I'll always love you. Always have and always will and nothing will ever change how I feel about you. Nothing."

Chapter 13

Joshua was sitting in the kitchen waiting for Jim to call when his uncle called to him. "Josh, what are you doing? Shouldn't boys your age be outside playing?"

"I'm waiting for an important phone call." Josh said as the phone rang. Stephen walked into the kitchen to answer it when he noticed Joshua already had. After saying hold on, Joshua covered the mouth piece to the phone and spoke to Stephen. "It's for me."

Stephen just shrugged his shoulders and walked away. How his nephew was so professionally business oriented was beyond him. He thought back to when he was Josh's age, he remembered listening to the Yankee's games on the radio with the family. Playing board games at the dining room table after dinner and dishes were done. But then he thought about all of the books he read as a child. Mystery stories about detectives and private eyes. He recalled all of the fun he had pretending he too was solving crimes. Maybe, in retrospect, his nephew was a lot like him, except he truly was trying to solve a mystery, not just find the neighbor's cat.

"Okay Joshua, what do I do?" Jim asked as he confirmed he was in Washington DC

"Okay, first NARA will tell you to check the regional facilities to verify that the information you're requesting isn't there."

"What is NARA?"

"National Archives & Records Administration." Joshua spoke assuming everyone knew the acronym. He learned it like four years ago.

"Sorry."

"If you can't find anything there, which I doubt you will since it was shipped over from another country, you will have to have the archives provide you access to all of the original records that were created and accumulated by Dr. Bizarro in the course of his life and daily business. Because these records usually can't be replaced, security will be tight. You'll need to request the following records and await their retrieval from the stacks. That list is written on a separate page, stapled inside the last journal I gave you.

Jim looked for the journal, found it and flipped to the back where he found the stapled paper. The first thing he saw was reference to a numbered journal and a page number. He recognized it. "This was mentioned in the first journal."

"That's right. I made a list of everything he put in separate journals that were referenced in the journals I had." Joshua admitted proudly.

"You are quite a detailed young man aren't you?" Jim asked proudly. He hoped one day he could be this proud of his own son or daughter… if they ever get the chance to have one.

"Once you sign in, they'll issue a researcher identification card, keep that safe. Then provide them a copy of the attached list and have them pull the crates for you. Then it's up to you to weed through all of the material and figure it out."

"I'm surprised you never found a way to do this yourself." Jim mused at how mature Joshua was for his age.

"You must be at least 14 years old or be accompanied by an adult, preferably a relative. In my case I don't make the age limits and my family would rather I stop looking into the past. They just want to forget about it."

"Well I can copy and mail you some of the journals that I find."

"That would be awesome. I would like that."

"Mail! Ugh, that takes like three days." Johnny complained. I couldn't wait that long. It's a good thing they've invented email now.

Grandma smiled. "It took a lot longer to deliver a letter back then."

"Really?" Jenny asked as she sat on the couch next to her Grandma petting the cat in her lap.

"Yes ma'am." Grandma spoke definitively then continued her story.

Ally had been sitting in her house for eight days solid. The week before Jim left they all decided it would be safer to stay in and Ally had been truly looking forward to a trip to the airport to send Jim off but he had an airport shuttle pick him up instead. Ally was getting claustrophobic. No one wanted her to go outside because of the reporters but Ally couldn't sit still much longer. She decided she wanted to go out and no one was going to stop her so she walked up to her father who was sitting at the table with a few of his new employees talking. Ally recognized George Sintel the bodyguard, she even recognized Samuel Swift her get away driver but even though she had seen the two women walking through the house she hadn't been properly introduced. She walked up to the table and spoke.

"Dad, George, Sam…" She greeted by first name then trailed off as she looked at the ladies. "I don't believe we've met." She said as she held out her hand to one of the two women. The first woman held out her hand and shook Ally's as she introduced herself.

"I'm Rachel Radcliff. Your father hired me to weed out the phone calls take care of the mailed correspondence etc." Then the second woman leaned forward and shook Ally's hand.

"And I'm Karen Shafer. I was hired to make the meals and do the upkeep with the house." Ally looked over at her father and grinned.

"The town's money sure came in handy didn't it?" She said with irritation.

"All necessities now darling." Bob said trying to help Ally understand.

"I see. Well I've got a necessity I'd like to take care of too."

"And what's that?" Her father asked.

"My need to go outside and enjoy the sunshine."

"No can do. Even though you can't see the reporters it doesn't mean they are not out there. We need to play it safe until Jim or the Doctor find a cure for you."

"I am not going to spend the rest of my life inside this house!" Ally began to yell.

"I'm not talking about the rest of your life, just until we figure this thing out." Bob tried to explain calmly.

"And what if we never figure it out? You know the town's money isn't going to last long the way you're spending it!"

"I don't deserve to be attacked." Her father demanded.

"And I don't deserve to be a prisoner in my own house!"

"Look Ally!" Bob began but was interrupted by George who stood up and interrupted the both of them.

"If I may Mr. Catsworth; you are paying me to protect your daughter, if she wants to go somewhere then please let me earn my money." Ally was shocked that George had sided with her and backed him up quickly.

"Yeah dad, let George earn his money."

"Ally…" Her father began to protest but knew it was a waste of breath. "Fine." Ally began to smile. "But this is an awful risk just for a little sunshine."

"Daddy, if I can't enjoy the day God gave me, then I might as well be dead."

"Well, that's grim." Bob began but Ally wasn't going to give him the chance to reconsider. She kissed him on the top of his head and ran off.

"Thanks dad, I'll be back soon. Come on George."

"Alright!" Johnny declared loudly as he sat up on his knees, "Now it's going to get good again."

"What do you mean?" Jenny asked curious as if she had missed something.

"Girls always get themselves in trouble. It's what they do." Johnny declared with so much certainty that Jenny simply had to protest.

"Hey! That's not true!"

"Really? Grandma said there was going to be death defying action today and I've waited long enough. She just has to get into trouble now!"

"Grandma, Ally's not going to get hurt is she?"

"No sweetheart, but unfortunately Johnny is right, something does happen to Ally."

"I knew it! Another mutant moment. This is so cool!"

"Do you think Ally or Jim thought it was cool?" Grandma asked curiously to get little Johnny thinking about this.

"Well of course not, but it was happening to them. It's never cool if bad things happen to you but when it happens to others..." Johnny trailed off realizing he was wrong. "Well no, it's not cool when bad things happen to others either."

Grandma smiled that he realized his mistake and was just about to start again when Johnny continued his thought. "But having mutant powers IS cool."

Grandma shook her head, looked up to the ceiling finding where she left off in her story and picked it back up again.

"The first morning Jim arrived at the National Archive building..."

"Hold-up Grandma!" Johnny stopped her, you went back to Jim and you were actually about to tell us how Ally gets cat-ified again."

"Cat-ified?" Grandma asked wondering where that word came from.

"Her DNA is being modified each time she turns into a cat so she is being cat-ified." Johnny spoke his thought so clearly Grandma couldn't help but agree.

"Well okay then. She'll become cat-ified in a moment, I wanted to tell you about Jim's progress first.

"Okay go on," Johnny groaned, but I really want to hear about the cat mutation stuff soon."

"Yes sir." Grandma smirked as she saluted her tough little soldier.

"That first morning Jim made it to the National Archive building. He registered and got his ID card and then a woman began informing him of the rules.

"You must leave all personal belongings in the free lockers. This includes bags, carrying cases, briefcases, purses, books, notebooks, and notepads. We will provide you with notepaper, note cards, and a pencil. Pens and highlighters are not allowed, nor are pressure sensitive notes, such as Post-its. Pre-written notes must be on loose paper not on a pad or in a notebook. Someone from our staff must stamp your notes to identify them as belonging to you. Stapled notes can be stamped once on the back. Pressure sensitive notes, such as Post-its, must be removed or stapled to the page. You may not bring items such as books, magazines, or newspapers unrelated to your research into the research room. Exceptions can be made at the discretion of the staff for materials closely related to your research. Once inside, you are responsible for safeguarding the condition of the records that have been brought to you. You may remove from a cart and open only one box or bound volume at a time. You may remove and open only one folder from a box at a time. The records should stay flat on the table at all times. The records must be kept in the same order in which they are given to you. If folders in a box or pages in a folder appear to be out of order, do not rearrange the records yourself. Alert the staff immediately. White gloves should be worn at all times when handling any paperwork, microfilm or motion picture records, to protect the records from oils or foreign contaminants. Any questions?"

"Plenty, but I'll think of them later." Jim said half joking, trying to find the humor in a situation where everything seemed so critical. The assistant didn't laugh. Then Jim followed a security guard down to the stacks. There he was given his pair of white gloves and told to wait in a room that was about the size of a small office. About twenty minutes later a forklift drove up with three crates. The forklift driver set the crates down in front of Jim and then waved goodbye.

"Wait! Are these all mine?" Jim asked with pure shock in his voice.

"Research papers by the late Doctor Bizarro volumes 1 through 3K, yup, all yours." As the forklift drove off Jim put his hand up to his face. He had expected he would get a lot of stuff, he just hadn't been expecting quite so much. He didn't know where to start, the job seemed so monumental, the task so difficult, but the reason for the job was so incredibly important to him that he knew he had to jump in and do this thing. It was up to him to find the cure for Ally, the love of his life, and that was a job he took exceptionally serious.

"Wow, he's going to be there for a REALLY long time!" Jenny exclaimed in sadness for Ally.

"Good! The more time for Ally to get cat-ified."

"Really Johnny?" Grandma asked.

"Well I'm right aren't I? She's going to get in trouble a lot while he's gone. Girls always do."

"Hey!" Jenny protested for all girls in general.

"We will have to have a talk about your view of women later," Grandma narrowed her eyes at Johnny knowing in her heart he just wanted to get to the action part of the story. He leaned back slightly with his shoulder raised when he saw his Grandma glaring at him. He realized he said something he shouldn't have so he said all he knew he could.

"Sorry."

Ally was dressed in a long dress covered with a dark shawl and had a big sun hat covering her face. She completed the look with sunglasses. She hardly recognized herself so she knew the reporters wouldn't recognize her either. They had driven to the park, just north of the town circle and were strolling down one of the finely manicured paths enjoying the day when Ally spoke to George, her bodyguard.

"I know that this is probably not the kind of job you signed up for. Baby sitting me as we walk through the park."

"The job is what it is." George admitted and then smiled a bit, "You know, people who need guarding are just regular people wanting to live regular lives most of the time. Some have been threatened for no fault of their own and just need protection. That's where I come in. I keep a look out for danger so you can just be yourself."

Ally smiled at that. She liked that he seemed to place her in the 'regular people' category as he spoke. It made her feel less like a freak. In fact, this entire outing had been just wonderful. Peaceful. Ally was just beginning to feel like things would be okay and go back to normal again soon, when…

The reporters had all gathered at Lone Prairie Diner for lunch, swapping stories and trying to figure out why they were really here when one of them spotted Ally and her bodyguard turn the corner.

"Hey! There they are!" One of the reporters called out. Everyone grabbed their equipment and cameras, threw money to the counter to pay their tabs in a hurry and rushed out the door. As soon as George saw the mob heading their way he told Ally to run and he grabbed her hand and led her across the park towards their car. When he realized that many of the reporters had jumped into their vans and were going to cut them off he came up with plan B. There was nowhere to run. They were coming from all directions. He changed directions, hand still held firm to Ally's hand as they ran towards the warehouse district just over the railroad tracks. He pulled Ally behind a building and spoke to her quickly.

"You run north, find a place to hide in that abandoned building over there and stay hidden until I find you. I'll draw their attention away from you and when they are off your scent I will come back for you. Got it?"

Ally followed George's directions and ran inside of the abandoned building. She watched George as he ran away yanking his jacket off his body, crumple it into a ball and pull it close to his torso, holding his crumpled jacket like he was holding a cat. It was quite smart she thought.

He ran somewhat towards the reporters, then turned right making them want to follow him. They chased him a good six blocks before he made the show that he wasn't carrying anything, especially not the infamous "Ally Cat." Once the reporters realized they had been had, most of them just dropped their hands and returned back to the diner where their food was getting cold. However a few of the reporters stuck with their gut feelings. Knowing something was up, they followed him, secretly. Like predators following prey they snuck behind George and followed him north down Main Street.

He had just turned the corner back into the alley to make his way to the abandoned building when he was nearly run over by a black van speeding out of the alley.

As it sped past him, he dove to the wall then turned to take in the details of the van.

Black van with black tinted windows and no license plates. He couldn't see inside. Had they apprehended Ally? He began to pursue when the abandoned building he told Ally to hide inside burst into flames with a roar and nearly knocked him off his feet. Not knowing whether Ally was in the van or the building George had to make a choice. It had only been a fraction of a second when he heard a reporter yell out for someone to call the fire department when it occurred to him; Ally had been sent many death threats in the mail lately.

There were all sorts of people writing all sorts of things about wanting her dead. There were cults worshiping her like the Egyptians to their cats, wanting to sacrifice her to their Gods. There were religious factions offering to exorcise the demon cat out of her. There were pagans explaining that fire was the only way to truly cleanse the world of this hell she was bringing into it. It was really morbid ideals mixed in with well wishes and scientific offerings, doctors offering their opinions and reporters offering her exclusives. Things like this seemed to bring out a whole slew of crazies and George was certain, one of those crazy parties were driving that van that had just sped away after setting an explosive charge in the building Ally had entered.

Certain now that Ally had to have been in that building, he ran towards it but was thrown off his feet again as another explosion propelled glass shards from the windows at him and the reporters, currently video taping the entire thing.

He got back to his feet and ran towards the building again but stopped when he heard her scream. As everyone looked up to see the broken shards of glass falling to the ground in front of them, George noticed a hand in an upstairs window sticking through the bars. It was Ally.

Ally was desperately trying to break free of the bared up window to no avail. The metal panels of the window pane just wouldn't break from the window frame. Realizing she couldn't get through them but seeing George below in the alley, looking up at her she screamed for him. She began to panic, feeling the souls of her shoes heat up from the fire below her and then smelling the smoke billow in through the only exit she saw in this room. She was screaming for help, and her screams seemed to echo downwards to the crowd of people gathering and ring in their ears as they all realized they were about to watch something bad happen.

The fire department drove up a moment later and five men jumped out of the truck, two to unravel the hose, two to get the water connected to the hydrant and one to raise the ladder as he realized everyone was looking up at the same broken window.

"There is a woman in that building!" One of the bystanders yelled and pointed. The fire department acted quickly.

Ally grabbed for the bars again trying to rattle them off but they had suddenly gotten too hot to touch. She screamed for help, turning to see the fire quickly approaching her from behind and knowing there was no way out through the bars.

"Not as a human." Johnny interjected.

"Shhh!" Jenny shushed him as she encouraged her Grandma to go on. They were both on the edge of their seats

-----

A loud explosion rocked the floor Ally was standing on and a blast of hot smoky air and fire created a wall of force that literally pushed her into the frame of the window. The weight of her body, the rattling of the explosion and the heat of the fire was enough to break the window frame free of the building and everyone watched as Ally was shoved out of the window as flames shot out from where she had just stood. There Ally fell four stories to the ground changing into a cat as she did.

George saw this and ran up to her the very second she landed, snatched her up into his arms and ran off before the reporters could even realize what they had just seen. He ran all of the way back to the house before Ally changed back to human and as he burst through the front door Karen Shafer and Rachel Radcliff ran up with towels and blankets and swept her from his arms. At first he was shocked that they were so well prepared but then he heard a police radio squawking from the dining room and realized that they had heard the call for help already. As George trotted into the kitchen, exhausted and still winded from his run he sat down at the kitchen table and dropped his head into his hands.

Bob walked into the room and saw George sitting there. "Where's Ally!"

"She's in her room with the ladies."
"What happened?"
"I'm sorry sir."
"How did she get out of your sight?"
"It was my fault sir. I take full responsibility."

Jim had been going through the first crate when he looked down at the pile he had already been through and then up at the mountain of journals he hadn't. The sudden realization that this would take forever engulfed him and he almost felt overwhelmed.. He didn't want to miss or skip over anything so he wanted to take his time going through these books, however, all of the work he did here had to be done during business hours and he couldn't work on it at night. He was grateful they allowed him to make copies so he could send them to Joshua but Joshua still hadn't received the first package and it had been over a week already.

By the time the day was over he was absolutely exhausted. Nearly falling asleep right where he sat, the guard had to come down and remind him to leave. They put his work away in proper order and left it there for him to pick up with tomorrow morning. Then they walked Jim out of the building and he walked to his hotel room. Once he got back to his room, he immediately plopped down on his bed and fell asleep.

About four o'clock in the morning Jim's hotel room phone rang and he answered it in his groggy state.

"I'm going to need pages 12 and 34 of journal 4 to further my research, if twelve is continued on then send me page thirteen as well. Also look for anything that says project W2. It's a whim but I think this has something to do with the DNA research."

"Joshua?" Jim asked realizing who was on the other end of the line.

"Yeah?"

"Jim squinted his eyes at his watch, "It's four in the morning. What are you doing up?"

"It's only 1:00 am here and your package arrived today. I've been studying it all night."

Jim sat up and grabbed a piece of paper and pen. "Which pages again?"

Joshua told him and then explained his thoughts on what he was expecting to find then changed the subject. "Have you seen the news?"

"No." Jim sat up suddenly filled with worry for Ally. He had come back to his hotel room and went straight to bed, he hadn't even called to check on her.

"She's fine." Joshua started with, "but she's on her seventh life now."

"What happened?"

Chapter 14

Once Jim knew everyone in the house would be awake he called.

"Catsworth residence."

"Rachel? It's Jim, how is Ally?"

"She is fine. George got her home safely and the burns aren't too serious."

"I heard about what happened I didn't see it."

"Oh." She paused then figured she needed to detail what happened. "She got caught in a building fire but she is okay. She lost another life leaping from the building and she got minor burns on her body but the doctor gave her a clean bill of health. Do you want me to wake her?"

"She's still asleep?"

"Yes. But I can wake her for you."

"No, that's all right, I'll call her later. Thank you." Jim really wanted to talk to her but he didn't want to wake her. As he hung up the phone he had just enough of this day and was ready for it to be over.

Jim had been so swept up in the research he had all but forgotten everything else of the world. He was sitting in a dark damp and dusty warehouse going through box after box of paperwork, journals and books for over a week now. The guard would come in and check on him every once in a while. There was no one who could help him and he wasn't allowed to take the items out of the warehouse. He sat Indian style on the cold hard cement floor and went through each and every page of paper one by one, writing down everything that could be useful or helpful

His only help was Joshua. Every thing he found he'd send to Joshua to peruse over and everything that seemed helpful Joshua made his notes on. Jim knew he was getting close to something, but he didn't know what it was yet. All he knew was Joshua believed time was running out for Ally and if Jim didn't find something soon he wouldn't have Ally to come home to, he'd have a cat, or nothing at all.

"What do you think is going to happen to her?" Jenny asked aloud. "Do you think she will turn into a cat and remain a cat forever or do you think she will just die after life nine."

"What makes you think she's even going to make it to life nine? I mean if that window frame wouldn't have given she would have been bar-be-que'd, grill marks and all!" Joshua expressed graphically.

"Shall we find out?" Grandma asked, which was enough to settle the children back down to listen.

Jim was quickly getting into his regimen. Research, report back to Joshua and then go back to his hotel and crash. He was completely emotionally, mentally and physically exhausted. The research was taking a lot out of him and it was showing through his wrinkled clothes, growing beard and mustache and the dark black circles under his eyes. Plus his lack of contact to Ally had kept him from being able to remember the true reason why he was going through all of this. He felt really guilty with the fact that he hadn't talked to her once since he had left. He had kept track of her whereabouts through Joshua and Rachel at the house but it just wasn't the same as being able to talk to her. That night he decided to call Ally just to see how she was doing and check up but when Rachel answered the phone she informed him Ally was asleep.

"Oh." Jim said with disappointment.

"Do you want me to wake her?"

Just then someone knocked at his door. He went to the peephole and looked through but saw no one. He waited a moment and then opened the door. Looking both left and then right down the hallway, he saw no one. He was just about to close the door when he saw a folded piece of paper on the floor. He stooped to pick it up and opened it. It said "One life left." Loosing his attention to Rachel on the phone he wondered about that. Joshua had said she was on life seven. To Jim, that meant she had two lives left, if he believed that hypothesis, which he didn't know if he did or not. So why would they say one life left?

"Jim? Are you still there?"

"Yeah, I've got to go."

"Is everything alright?"

"Fine."

"Did you want me to wake Ally?" Rachel asked again but Jim's attention was lost on this query.

"No, I'll just talk to her another time." He said blindly as he began writing down a list of lives that he knew about.

"I don't understand, Grandma. What's wrong?" Johnny asked wondering what was so important about the number of lives.

"Well, lets figure it out." Grandma said as she stood and grabbed a pad of paper, tearing off a sheet for both Johnny and Jenny and grabbing two pencils. "How many lives has she been through?"

"Seven." Both kids agreed.

"Write them down. In order as they happened." Grandma insisted so they did.

As Jenny kept writing, Johnny paused and looked onto Jenny's paper, "you forgot the hospital."

"What hospital?"

"Where they had her tied down, it came after that one you wrote was the fight with Jim and she saw her whiskers in the mirror."

"Oh right." They both looked at Jenny's list. Jenny put sequential numbers next to each and then showed her Grandma. "See, there were only seven changes. Seven lives."

"That's what Jim thought a moment ago, but what if he was wrong?"

"What do you mean Grandma?"

"What if the waterfall you have marked as number one, was actually the end of her first life, so that would actually begin life two?" Jenny and Johnny stared at the paper and thought about it and slowly, Jenny, scratched out the number one and put number two and then changed the rest of the numbers in order leaving the number eight in front of the burning building.

"Oh no. She only has one life left!"

"Not really. This just means that she might be beginning life eight. She may still have all of life eight and then all of life nine."

"So she still has two lives left?"

"If she was on life seven, she would have three lives left, but if she's on life eight, then she only has two."

"That's confusing. How do we know?"

"That's the problem. No one knew. No one knew which life she was really on because they had all been guessing up until now, so they didn't know whether she had two or three left.

"But wait! The note Jim received said one life left."

"That's right" She agreed.

"But you just said it was either two or three."

"I said she *may* have two or three. That was assuming she doesn't die *on* life nine."

"Huh?" The kids spoke in unison.

"Does she die *on* life nine, or *after* life nine?"

"After."

"On."

Both kids looked at each other like they were wrong. Then they looked back up at their Grandma confused. "Stand up both of you. Turn around, and when I count to three, jump."

"Ok."

"1, 2, 3."

Johnny jumped on three, Jenny jumped after.

"Why did you go early?" Jenny asked.

"Why did you jump late?" Johnny came back.

"You see children, it's all a matter of perspective. No one is either right *or* wrong. Since there is someone much higher than all of them making these rules for Ally,"

"You mean God?"

Grandma nodded and continued, "they wouldn't know until the final moment which it had been."

"So the next time she changes she could really die?" Johnny inquired with so much concern, Grandma thought he was going to cry.

"They didn't know. Depending on how you looked at it, she could have three, two or only one life left."

"Wow. That's confusing." Johnny admitted as he tried to wrap his head around it.

"Here's something else to add to that confusion." Grandma added. "There was no way to prove if the nine life theory was really happening. Each time she turned she was changing her DNA, that's all they knew and they were grasping onto some old wives tale about nine lives hoping they had more time."

"Wives tail?" Jenny asked confused.

"It's a term meaning an old story."

"So wives don't have tails?" Jenny clarified. Grandma laughed.

"So as you can see, she might have one life or three or they may be wrong about the nine lives all together and it could be something entirely different."

"Wow. Ally has some major problems." Johnny scowled.

"That she did."

Chapter 15

As Jim flipped through page after page of journal entries he suddenly noticed something that seemed to be out of place. He pulled out the folded piece of paper and unfolded it. It was a picture; a hand drawn picture in crayon of a young girl holding hands with an older man wearing a white lab coat. It looked like a four-year-old child had drawn it. The child's writing above the people in the picture said "me and daddy". Suddenly Jim realized he had a clue. Sophia had drawn this; Joshua's aunt, but more importantly, it was the same paper type as his journals but up until now, it wasn't torn out of any journals he or Joshua had gone through. There was another journal.

Ally had just finished breakfast and was staring out the back window of the house when she caught a glimpse of her reflection in the glass. Her face, her actions were still all over the tabloids and news. She cried. She prayed for this mess to end and she prayed she would have the strength to see it through.

Bob was sitting downstairs watching the news with George just shaking his head. Ally was the story of the century and the only thing accomplished by allowing her to go to town was to remind the press just how exciting it was to follow Ally around and hope they caught her changing into a cat again.

Joshua had been mulling over the note Jim told him about receiving, for hours now. He too found the situation confusing. Was Ally at life seven or eight? Did she have three lives left or one. The whole nine lives theory came from the hypnotist and it was feasible with all of the doors Ally had described, but since she hadn't gone into each door, they really didn't know for sure. Unfortunately, after Dr. Shiltz had broken doctor patient confidentiality and told the news about his findings and how she changed into a cat in his office, he had been disbarred and Jim and Ally had vowed to never go back to another hypnotist again.

Unfortunately, Joshua couldn't find a way around it. Another walk down her hallways would answer so many questions about her past lives and about the nine life theory and there was a possibility if she were to be able to learn more at the lab that night she might be able to see the missing journal he and Jim were now sure existed.

"This is Rachel Radcliff, how may I direct your call?"

At first Joshua was confused. He had dialed the number Ally & Jim gave him, but he thought it sounded like it was a work place rather than their home phone number.

"Hello?" The receptionist repeated.

"Um, is Ally there?" Joshua asked with shyness.

"Who may I say is calling?"

"Is this a business?"

"No, I am the receptionist for the Brooks residence. And you are?"

"I am Joshua, a friend of Ally's."

"Is she expecting your call?"

"No, because I haven't had a chance to talk to her yet."

"You said your name was…"

"Joshua Laden, her friend in New York."

"Okay, let me see if she is available."

Joshua was nearly laughing at the silliness of the situation when Ally picked up the phone.

"Joshua?"

"Ally, how are you doing?"

"I'm going nuts here. My father's hired a bodyguard, receptionist, maid and personal driver; it's all I can do to get a little peace and quiet."

"I see." Joshua sighed.

"I'm sorry, you didn't call to hear me gripe did you?"

"It's alright." Joshua added then got serious. "Listen some things have come up here that I need to get more information on, but I can't do it here. Uncle Stephen said it was okay if I come for a visit, so how does your schedule look?"

"I'm open. What's going on?"

"Nothing I want to discuss over the phone. I'll see you soon."

"You want me to send my driver to pick you up?"

"Are you serious?" Joshua smirked.

"I just wanted to say it. I can send Sam to pick you up at the airport, just forward your itinerary to my receptionist."

"You are having way too much fun with this." Joshua laughed. Ally burst out laughing.

"Hey, this is the most fun I've had since I went to Hollywood."

"At least you *went* to Hollywood."

As Joshua thought about it, he loved the idea. "*Could* you send Sam to pick me up?"

"I don't see why not. You said you have Stephen's permission?"

"Of course."

"Then I'll put him on the phone and you two can work on the details."

"Thanks Ally! You're the best!"

"Oooh, I'll bet he really didn't have permission." Johnny spoke up quick.

"What makes you think that?" Grandma smiled.

"He's ten years old. Ten year olds don't travel without their parents."

"Some travel without their parents, but they have permission to do so."

"Yeah but Joshua isn't coming on a plane, he's having Ally's driver pick him up in New York. That sounds shady."

"Maybe he was saving money for plane fair." Jenny added.

"Yeah, like his aunt or uncle would be okay with driving off with some stranger on his own."

"We'll see." Grandma cooed and continued.

"Mr. Laden?" The rather tall man spoke. Joshua looked up at him and smiled.

"Are you Sam?"

"Samuel Swift, the Brooks personal valet." He said as he stuck out his hand to shake. "Good to meet you sir."

Joshua found it incredibly nice to have a personal valet; the man helped him with his bag, drove all the way and walked him into the house. There, Joshua was greeted by the receptionist.

"Mr. Laden, I'm Rachel Radcliff, if you need anything, anything at all just let me know."

"Okay, I will." Joshua smiled as she led him upstairs to his room. She showed him around and then announced that Ally would by right in to see him. A short time later, Ally walked in and they both hugged.

"Joshua, how good it is to see you again. How was your trip?"

"Good."

"So, why did your uncle allow this?" Ally jumped right into the questions.

"It's pretty easy when he thinks I'm in Science camp."

"Joshua! You didn't tell him you were coming here?"

"Like he would have let me come. Besides, we're getting close to something and I didn't think it could wait."

"Like what?" Ally asked curiously.

"Like..." Joshua paused collecting his thoughts. "Like, Ally, how would you feel about going to see another hypnotist?"

"What? Where did that come from?"

"I know your last visit went unbearably bad, but there have been a few things brought to my attention recently that I can only get explanation about from you, your past lifes."

"Joshua, I don't know..." Ally hesitated.

"Just hear me out. If you still feel hesitant about it, then tell me no and I will think of something else."

"Okay Joshua, I'm all ears." Ally smiled as she sat down ready for a good story.

A months worth of research 9 hours a day Jim finally made it through every journal Dr. Bizarro had. He knew one thing through all of this research that there was at least one journal unaccounted for and it didn't exist in the National Archives. As he packed up his things and looked around the dusty dark warehouse he knew one thing - he would not miss this place.

"Do you really believe that?" Ally interrupted as Joshua finished up his explanation.

"I know that my grandfather was that scientist, and that you are connected through reincarnation to his lab assistant. You getting hypnotized one more time could help answer so many of those questions that only you, as the lab assistant can answer. If I could find the man reincarnated from my grandfather I would ask him but I can't find him. So Ally, please, would you do it?"

"Well, we'll need to find a respectable hypnotist, make an appointment, we don't know if he or she will even have an opening for us this week."

"I am already one step ahead of you." Joshua smiled proudly. "I contacted Doctor Roberts two days ago and got a recommendation. I checked out this woman's credentials and then made an appointment. We're scheduled for three tomorrow afternoon."

"And what if I would have said no?" Ally smiled.

"I would have canceled the appointment." Joshua spoke matter of factly. "But I had a good feeling you wouldn't have."

"You are a very smart kid, uh, young man, you know that?" Ally smiled.

"Thank you."

The next day Ally, Joshua, George Sintel the bodyguard and Samuel Swift the driver went to go see Dr. Julia Newton the new hypnotist. Ally's father was very much against the whole idea of going out, seeing another hypnotist and risking the exposure but he couldn't stop his daughter, especially with all of the extra help he had hired for just such an occasion.

He did however make sure that there would be plenty of protection around her just in case she was recognized.

Ten minutes till three the car pulled up in front of the hypnotists building. George the bodyguard got out first and opened Ally's door, quickly scanning the street for any potential dangers. Then he walked Ally and Joshua in, making sure Sam the driver stayed in the car, ready to go in a hurry just in case. Once they met up with the new hypnotist and George checked the office over, he left them to their business and stood guard outside the office door.

"All right Ally, you've done this before." Dr. Julia Newton explained as she sat down on a chair in front of Ally's seat. "Let's get right into it, according to your friend Joshua we have a lot of work to do here in a very short amount of time. Are you ready?"

"Yes."

"Good. Close your eyes. Take a deep breath and relax. Clear your mind of everything and listen only to my voice. When I say five, begin to exhale slowly as I count down. Ready?"

"Mmhmm." Ally hummed her readiness.

"Okay. Inhale." Ally did. She inhaled deeply and then waited. "Five." Then Ally exhaled slowly. The hypnotist counted backwards from five very slowly and Ally felt herself quickly going to sleep. A few moments later, Dr. Newton spoke again.

"Okay Ally, you are in a dark tunnel, it's the tunnel of your life. Go down the," She paused as she looked over Joshua's notes. "The left hallway." The doctor then looked at Joshua, "Is this research correct?"

"Yes. She has at least two hallways which is odd I know. She's been hypnotized before and this is what they found. I got a transcript from the other doctor."

"Okay."

"Can I say something?" Ally spoke quick.

"Of course, Ally," the doctor chimed, "What is it?"

"There are now seventeen doors."

"Wait!" Joshua jumped, "there were fifteen last time, right?"

"Right." Ally confirmed.

"Then this confirms it, each time she transforms into a cat she is using up a cats life."

"I'm still lost." Ally spoke, the math doesn't figure."

Joshua spoke aloud, "Well, lets do the math: life one and two were human, second life ended when you were turned into a cat from the lab, then nine lives as a cat makes eleven lives, then this life as a human makes twelve and the first time you were hypnotized you said there were fifteen doors and you had turned into a cat twice by then? So it works out that life eleven was broken off for the nine cat lives. So seventeen doors means three more lives used up for a total of six lives, you're on life seven and after that you have two to go."

"But I've turned more times than that…"

"But was each turn life threatening or just emotional?"

"Emotional?" Ally considered it and then

sighed. "Oh that's a relief."

"Alright Ally," the doctor chimed in, "Lets get back to it. Enter into the second door to the left and tell us what you see."

For the next hour the three of them discovered the many lives of Goldie the cat. She had been injected with the serum, which had turned her into a cat. Once the transformation had taken place everything went blurry. The feline, in her freaked-out state, ran through the lab accidentally knocking over a lantern, which began a fire. The fire quickly over took the place within minutes and she escaped out of the burning science lab through the window. She actually went through one life just getting out of there. Her second life began immediately after; she was nearly hit by a car as she ran across the street to get to safety. The third life was used up trying to find Dr. Bizarro the next morning but he was being held in jail, and she couldn't get to him. She overheard from outside the barred window every word he said as he called his brother for help.

"James, brother, I need your help." Auguste said as he waited for James' response. "What do you mean you don't care? I am your brother!" He paused to listen to James again. "But you don't understand the experiment worked! It was a success!"

Goldie the cat listened to the conversation closely, understanding every word, every sigh and every plea. She could tell that Auguste's brother didn't believe him about the accident but he kept trying to convince him. As one of the officers approached him, letting Auguste know his time was just about up, Auguste interrupted his brother for the last part.

"Listen, believe me or not, but there is one sure way to prove my innocence! Find Goldie, she is an orange cat now, but I think she will be trying to find me. In my apartment there is a hidden journal. There is one thing written in it, the formula used to transform her. I am positive that if you recreate the formula, but replace the nepeta cataria oil with the sebum oil formulation in the journal and inject her with it, it will turn her human again. It is the only thing that can be done to prove my innocence. Will you do that for me?" He waited for James' response. "Please brother. I know it sounds crazy but it's the truth!" He listened to his brother for another moment. "I don't know how you will find Goldie, but you must." He paused again. "No I don't know how many orange cats there are in the city!"

Goldie realized immediately that if she wanted to be human again she would need to find James directly. She knew that his house was forty miles outside of the city in a little country town and she knew it would be a long a difficult trip to get there, but she knew without a shadow of a doubt that she must find him no matter what the cost. She wasn't only saving her life, but Auguste's as well.

The hypnotist had Ally go into her next life but after a brief glance in the door she could see that Goldie was still on her trek to James. She skipped to the next life and found Goldie the cat walking up to a large house in the country. She immediately realized that Goldie had gone through two lives just getting to him and she knew that the determination and love Goldie had for Auguste and herself was strong.

"Okay Ally, describe the scene to me." Doctor Newton spoke.

"I'm sitting outside of James' living room window. He is talking to himself I think, I don't see anyone else in the room."

"What is he saying? Can you hear him?"

"He's ranting about Auguste, how crazy he is."

"Has he got the journal?"

"It could be the journal on his desk. He keeps pacing back and forth and having this conversation, saying, "Sure brother I'll help you. I'll show the world that I am just as crazy as you are because I believe some mixed liquid can turn a human into a cat. Then I'll loose my business, all of my clients, my home, my family, my life. Sure I don't have anything better to do now than look after what you've left behind. It's not like my life was boring or non eventful before. And sure, this search for an orange cat, that's simple, why? Because she'll just walk right up to me and say, hey, I'm Goldie, mind changing me back? Am I really that naïve? He killed her, simple as that. Why? I don't know. He didn't want her to tell the world he was a quack maybe. That makes more sense than this." He picked up the journal and nearly threw it in the fireplace but paused. He started at it for a moment, then decided to slip it into his desk drawer.

Goldie immediately realized that her life would soon be over if she didn't convince James of the truth. She ran to the window nearest to him and began pawing at it and meowing loudly. James at first ignored her, but she continued, finally he looked at her and for a moment, she felt he knew who she was. But within moments he turned. He yelled at her. "Go away! Leave me alone!" Goldie persisted nevertheless. She scratched at the window with her claws, tearing at the glass, screeching loudly, echoing in the room. It seemed as if James were going nuts. He grabbed his ears with his hands and clasped them shut, he squeezed his eyes closed and began to yell. "This isn't happening! This isn't true!"

Goldie continued to meow, screaming at the top of her feline lungs to get James' attention and slowly he began to calm. He took his hands from his ears and slowly opened his eyes. He stared at the orange cat sitting outside of his window for the longest moment and Goldie stared back, wondering if he could just see into her eyes, into her soul, if he would be able to see who she really was. He slowly turned and went back to his desk. He opened a drawer and pulled something out. Goldie thought it was a key to the door and her heart jumped for joy at the prospect of finally getting through to him. She waited patiently. Smiled a feline smile. Knew in her heart that everything would be fine now. When James turned back around and faced her.

She saw it in her hand but it didn't seem right. She must not be seeing it right. At first she was confused, shocked, she couldn't figure out what he was doing or thinking. "He can't be." She thought as she watched in slow motion as he pulled the trigger back. She turned on her heels as fast as she could, she started to scramble but couldn't find traction.

"He's got a gun!" Ally yelled.

"Get out of there, go through the door now Ally!" The hypnotist yelled as fast as she could. She stood. Joshua stood. They waited, with bated breath, waited for Ally to respond. Their hearts were pounding in their chest. Joshua could feel his pulse beating his rib cage.

"He shot at me. As I left the room, I even heard a second shot."

Doctor Newton and Joshua both fell back down into their chairs exhaling deeply. "Thank God!" Newton spoke as she looked back down at her notes. "Thank God you're safe Ally. I didn't realize we had gotten so close to the end of that life."

"Bizarro's own brother tried to eliminate the evidence. What a…" Ally began to cuss but was interrupted by Joshua.

"So he threw away the journal?"

"I don't know if it was the right one, but the journal he had he placed in his desk drawer.

Chapter 16

"Holy cow! This is getting deep!" Johnny spoke up loudly.

"So The scientists' brother didn't believe him?" Jenny asked of her grandmother.

"No, he was trying to hide the truth. It was some big conspiracy, wasn't it Grandma?" Johnny threw in his thoughts.

Grandma smiled looking at the two of them, sitting up on their knees in front of her, their eyes open so wide, the gears in their brains just churning away at the information. It was amazing to see the lights in their eyes so bright.

"She wants us to be quiet so she can finish." Jenny said to Johnny then glanced back up at her Grandma to make sure she was right. She saw her Grandma smile at her with a wink in her eye and then looked back at Johnny to gloat.

"Well okay then, please Grandma, can you continue?"

After all that Ally had been through today and the past few months she was desperately in need of some peace. She needed to get away from all of the people, the reporters the psychos and the bodyguards, and most of all she had to get out of this house. Even for just an hour or two, she needed some alone time. She needed to be somewhere she couldn't hear the entire household talking. She knew they couldn't be talking about her all of the time, but nevertheless they were talking, mumbling, even rambling by the time the echoing sounds of all of their voices made it upstairs and into her room. It was unnerving not having any quiet to herself. How could she think with all of this noise? How could she rest knowing the proof, the solution to all of this was in a journal that had been thrown away.

And Jim, her loving husband had been gone for so long already, researching, going through all of Bizarro's research at the archives for what? Nothing! What he was looking for wasn't there after all. If that first hypnotist wouldn't have broken doctor patient confidentiality she would have gone back for a second meeting. They would have found this out weeks ago. They could have avoided all of those deadly situations, the reporters wouldn't have had more to publicize. Ally was so angry she could claw someone's eyes out. Was that a cat reference? She was even beginning to think like a cat, she scolded herself. Maybe she *was* going crazy.

She was so tired of it all. After weeks of nonstop chatter from the people, the TV, the phones ringing and the radios blaring Ally knew she had to get out of here or she would go completely crazy. So after receiving her dinner that night she told Rachael that she wanted to be left alone the rest of the evening, and once everything seemed clear, Ally opened up her bedroom window and snuck out.

Ally had just made it out of the house safely and was trying to decide where to go when she heard something from across the street. She glared through the darkness towards the sound but saw nothing. She glared into the darkness for just a few moments longer and suddenly her eyes focused in on something. A black van, parked in a back alleyway. Its lights and engines were off and there was no motion. She watched it for a moment longer, listening, nothing. So Ally came to the conclusion that the van was not what she had heard but she found it oddly interesting that she was able to see this black van in the black of night without a flashlight.

Ally knew it wasn't safe out here for her by herself, it seemed every reporter and whack job wanted to get a piece of her and she knew it, but for some reason she felt she was willing to risk it all for just a short time to herself. Was she insane? To walk alone, at night, without letting anyone know where she was going. She was acting completely irrational and irresponsible. Maybe she should go back. What had she been thinking?

She turned and began walking back towards the house when she heard something again. She turned to see what it was but again saw nothing moving, the van was still in the same place nothing seemed out of place. Suddenly Ally felt like this moment of peace was too dangerous. She wasn't sure if her father and everyone had gotten to her, making her believe it wasn't safe now without a bodyguard, or if her feline senses detected trouble, all she knew was she needed to get back inside; quick.

Ally was rushing back down the sidewalk to her house, when she heard something else, a vehicle, but by now she was too frightened to look back. Little did she know but a faction of people who were anti-supernatural had been staking out her home and when they saw her sneak out the back they decided to make their move. They ran up behind her, grabbed her and before she could scream or even change, they covered her face with a damp cloth of Ether and waited for her to pass out. Before she knew it, she was blacking out and her body was being thrown into the back of the black van she had been so interested in a short moment ago.

"Cat-napped!" Johnny leaped into the air. "This is awesome!"

"Awesome? She's just been kidnapped and no one even knows she's missing!" Jenny exclaimed upset.

"She can take care of herself."

"She's out cold. She can't do anything!"

"But…" Johnny paused, "She'll be okay, right Grandma?"

"I'm home!" Jim exclaimed as he walked in through the front door. Everyone in the household showed their excitement in seeing him. They all welcomed him back, hugged him and helped him out with his bags. Everyone asked him how the trip went what he had found out but all Jim wanted to do at this exact moment was see Ally. He knew he should be more sociable but there were only two things on his mind, see Ally and get some rest. Bob, Ally's father told him Ally was already asleep upstairs, but she wouldn't mind Jim waking her. Jim smiled and went upstairs. He quietly opened the door to her darkened bedroom and walked in.

"Ally, I'm home." He whispered lovingly. She didn't stir. He walked up to the side of the bed and pressed his hand upon her shoulder. "Ally." But he quickly realized that it wasn't Ally's shoulder he was touching and he turned on the light. He flung back the blanket on the bed to see two pillows laid out like a sleeping body under the covers. He looked around the room and saw the window upon and he knew immediately something was wrong. Jim ran downstairs as fast as he could and yelled.

"Ally's not in her room. Are you sure she was supposed to be there?"

"Yes, that's where she said she would be the rest of the night."

"Well, she's not there any more. Check the house."

"Yes sir!" A couple of people said as they ran in different directions. Bob walked up to Jim and spoke.

"Things have been crazy around here, there is always so much going on."

"Would she have gone outside? Her bedroom window was open."

"I don't think so, that would be suicide with all of the reporters and..." Just then the receptionist yelled down to them from the top of the stairs, "She's not upstairs." The maid ran in from the kitchen, "She's not in here either!" Then George the bodyguard ran into the room.

"She's missing!" Panic loomed in the house as everyone yelled out questions.

"How long has she been gone? Who was the last person to see her? Where would she go? Was there any reporters or strange vehicles outside? Did she walk, did she drive? Was she taken?"

"Just find her!" Jim yelled frantically.

When Ally finally woke up she found herself sitting on a chair on top of a wooden platform, her hands were tied behind her back. There was chanting all around her but she couldn't see who it was who had captured her through the dim light of fiery torches and dark night sky. She could tell by the light wind rustling through leaves of the trees that she was somewhere in the woods, possibly the park but she couldn't see the night sky through the tree tops to get an idea of where she was at.

"Where am I?" She demanded angrily upset that she had been kidnapped and tied up.

"Where all judgments will be determined and punishment doled out." A deep scratchy voice boomed from behind a torch directly in front of her. Slowly her eyes adapted to what light there was and she was able to see the heavily bearded face of the man who had just spoke to her.

"What?" Ally asked as she looked around the platform and realized there was a noose wrapped around her neck. The men seemed to be chanting around the platform, Ally couldn't tell what they were saying, she figured they were speaking in old Latin, but what few words she could understand were things like, "inhumanus" meaning non-human, "monstrum" meaning monster and "morieris" which meant die. Ally feared what they were about to do when one of the men reached over and began to pull the latch.

"Wait! Why are you doing this?" Ally cried.

"You are not of this world. Your witch-like ability makes you evil and it's our duty as the master race to eliminate your supernatural kind from our world."

"I'm not evil! I haven't done anything wrong!"

"Do you deny your subhuman transformation into a feline?"

"Yes!"

"So you are not the one who has turned into a cat?" The leader asked with confusion.

Ally hated the idea of lying but she felt no other choice, maybe if she were able to convince these people that she wasn't the woman they were looking for, maybe they'd let her go. Of course she was being extremely optimistic. She wasn't naïve, she had a good feeling that even if she were able to convince them she wasn't their intended they would still kill her just because she knew who they were. But at the moment she had to keep her mind clear and calm, and she had to figure out how to get out of this.

"No, I am not the woman you think I am!"

"Gee, guys, looks like we got the wrong woman. What should we do?" The leader of the group spoke out looking around to his men. They all laughed wickedly and then one man spoke.

"We should give her the test!"

"You are absolutely right. We will submit the test." The leader spoke up brightly.

"What is the test?" Ally asked cautiously, knowing whatever it was, it wasn't good.

"It's simple. We go ahead with our plan and hang you. If you die, then you aren't the woman we thought you were and we'll apologize." The leader explained.

"We're not in Salem! And I'm not a witch! You can't do this to me!" Ally cried.

"We understand the idea of dying is not very appealing to most and we feel for your predicament but it is our duty to rid the world of evil so we must administer the test. Are there any last words you'd like to share?"

"I hope the police find you all and put you behind bars where you belong!"

Just then one of the men pulled the latch and Ally felt her stomach jump to her throat as she fell through the trap door. Fear overwhelmed her entire body in a flash. Before they knew it she had transformed into a cat, her dress was floating to the ground as the gold cat hanging in the noose used its claws to shred the rope above her. Finally the rope snapped and she fell free. She scrambled into the woods as fast as her furry little legs could take her. The rope remaining around her neck got caught on many bush branches and rocks, yanking her backwards as she ran and she began realizing what a dog must feel like on a leash, but she kept running nevertheless until she was all the way home.

She was absolutely exhausted as she turned the corner to her street but her emotions heightened when she saw Jim. He was out looking for her, standing in the middle of the sidewalk looking into the bushes. He was definitely a sight for sore eyes Ally thought as she ran right up to him and hopped into his arms before he even realized what was happening. At first he was shocked that a cat leapt into his arms, then he realized who it was and he began to calm down. However once his mind caught up to the situation he realized that Ally had been in another life threatening situation and had wasted another life. Once Ally felt safe, she began to change back to her human self. However, the noose was still tied around her neck and as she began to grow into her human form, the ropes began to tighten around her neck. Choking and freaking out, she quickly changed back into a cat just long enough for Jim to realize and remove the noose from around Ally's neck. As he took the noose with both hands ripping it off from her neck, Ally fell to the ground, changing as she did to land on her human feet but quickly loosing her balance and fainting. Jim caught her in his arms and looked at her.

Jim noticed she wasn't hurt or bleeding and at first found her greeting quite moving and formal for a man who had been away from the love of his life for so long, but then he realized, Ally was standing outside naked and it wasn't just because she was happy to see him. He quickly removed his jacket and wrapped it around her covering her naked body with it. He didn't know what happened to her just now but he knew she would fill him in soon. As for right now he knew he had to get her inside before anyone else saw them. It just wasn't safe out here for her and he knew it!

As they walked into the house everyone rejoiced in excitement to see the two of them but the sight of Ally wearing nothing but Jim's coat informed them she had been through another life threatening situation and as they noticed the swelling and redness around her neck, they knew it was something bad. They all wanted to ask her about it, but they could see by the expression on her face that she couldn't talk about it just now. Bob ran into the kitchen and grabbed a syringe and vail for Jim to take Ally's blood, and he handed it to Jim as he walked Ally upstairs, but nothing was said. They all knew their job and they all knew they didn't have to talk about it. Jim then took Ally upstairs as the rest of the family just tried to stay quiet and out of the way.

Once Jim got Ally upstairs and laid her down in bed he sat next to her and sighed. "I know that

I've been gone for a while and that I haven't called you so I don't claim to know what all has been going on here, but I don't think I'm off base asking you why."

"I know it was stupid of me to sneak out but I had to. I was getting so claustrophobic. I had begged and pleaded to go out a week ago. I had given all of my best arguments until I was allowed to go and even then I was forced to go with George and even with protection I was caught in a building fire."

"I heard about that."

"So I knew that if I asked again the answer would be definitely not."

"But you couldn't accept that?"

"I thought that maybe if I went out at night time that no one would see me, that the darkness would hide me better, that most of the reporters would be asleep."

"But?"

"But I didn't expect those men to be watching the place."

"Who were they? What did they want?"

"They wanted me dead. They said I was evil and needed to be extinguished from the planet." Just then George walked into the room, he had come in to apologize for not being more aware and to see how Ally was doing when he heard something even more important. Ally had continued her story of what had happened to her tonight and it all began to make sense. "All I know is they came up behind me, before I could do anything they covered my nose and mouth with a cloth and before I blacked out from the chemicals I saw them haul me into a black van.

"A black van?" George spoke up.

"Yes. I saw it through the darkness before they grabbed me, it was a black delivery van with no license plate."

"Good, very good." George exclaimed. Jim stood up with curiosity.

"What is it George?"

"Witnesses as well as myself noticed a black Chevy van with tinted windows speeding away from the building on main moments before the building caught on fire."

"You think these men are the same men who started the fire?" Ally asked.

"I do. At least now I can take care of one potential threat and get these whacko's off the street once and for all." George walked out of the room towards the kitchen phone and dialed the police.

Now that Joshua was back at home he went to his Uncle Stephen and Aunt Sophia to talk. "I know I shouldn't have lied about where I went."

"No you shouldn't have."

"But it was for a good reason."

"There is never a good reason to lie."

"But I know you wouldn't have let me go!"

"No we wouldn't have." Aunt Sophia spoke, "But we would have let you call Ally."

"I needed to be there."

"Joshua, you sound as if you are trying to defend your actions, not rectify them." Stephen scolded.

"But I did find something out."

"I don't care…" Stephen began but Sophia gave in.

"What did you find out Josh?"

"Grandpa Bizarro's brother James killed Goldie Givens."

"What?" Both adults spoke in unison.

"Well the cat Goldie."

"Oh not this again!" Stephen threw his hands in the air.

"It's true! Goldie Givens WAS transformed into a cat and she DID try to contact James for help after hearing Bizarro call him from the police station but James pulled a gun on her and shot her instead."

"This is ridiculous." Stephen announced with annoyance.

"What is?"

"Okay, even if Bizarro would have been able to transform Goldie into a cat, why would James want to help him out?"

"Because they were brothers."

"Bizarro was helping Hitler!"

"So?" Joshua asked not able to understand why Stephen was so angry.

"Tell me Joshua, what do you know of World War Two?"

"It was bad. Hitler had lots of Jewish people killed in the Holocaust. The atomic bomb was created, killing even more. Japan had kamikaze pilots who killed themselves in order to kill others. There was Pearl Harbor and dozens of other battles all over the world, it was all really bad."

"You think that was bad? When World War II ended in 1945, the entire Jewish secular and religious culture in Europe had been obliterated, and about six million Jews had been exterminated and over a million of the victims were children. The Nazis murdered some 3.5 million captured Soviet soldiers, mainly by starvation but also by shooting and gassing, in prisoner-of-war camps, slave labor facilities, and concentration camps. In the fall of 1939 they started their euthanasia program, in which Nazi doctors murdered the mentally and physically disabled people too. They were weeding out everyone who wasn't a pure German, an Aryan!"

"I know this!" Joshua yelled.

"Well imagine how many more millions he would have succeeded in killing if he would have gotten that formula!"

"What?" Joshua asked with confusion, he didn't understand what World War Two had to do with Goldie and Ally. His Uncle continued.

"In August 1940 the Germans launched daylight raids against ports and airfields and in September against inland cities. The objective was to draw out the British fighters and destroy them. However, the Germans failed to reckon with a new device, radar, which greatly increased the British fighters' effectiveness. Because their own losses were too high, the Germans had to switch to night bombing but when Bizarro's work failed to succeed

Hitler had to postpone the invasion indefinitely, thereby conceding defeat in the Battle of Britain. Just imagine what he would have been able to do if he would have overtaken Britain? And he could have with Bizarro's formula for superior soldiers! Imagine what the world would think about the Bizarro's then, the scientist who helped Hitler take over the world. James did the world a favor by letting Bizarro rot in prison."

"He was flesh and blood family!"

"He was a nut and deserved to die for taking that job!"

"Okay fine! He took a job that he shouldn't have, and he died for it! The formula never got into Hitler's hands and Hitler committed suicide so he can't get it now. So now that there isn't any more threat why can't we figure this out so we can save Ally?"

"Who?"

"Allison Catsworth."

"The freak?"

"The woman who can turn into a cat, yes. The woman who was reincarnated from Goldie Givens, the same Goldie Givens that was transformed into a cat by Bizarro's formula."

"Even if I had the journal, I doubt it would help her."

"Why?"

"Because this is ridiculous."

Finally Sophia spoke up. "What do you think is in this journal that would help Mrs. Catsworth?"

"He claims that the formula is written in one place and one place only, that journal."

"And James had it last?"

"He put it in his desk drawer just before he tried to gun down Goldie the cat."

"I think I remember that day." Sophia mulled quietly. "Auguste, my father was already in jail for murder. I was staying with his brother James. I remember a day that I heard gun shots, but he told me he had seen a snake in the house and shot it."

"You were there that day? Did you see the journal?"

"Please excuse me, Joshua. I need to look into something.

The next morning Jim took Ally to see Dr. Roberts. He hadn't seen them since Ally's last change but each time he saw her he could tell things were only getting worse. He checked the DNA strands in the new vail of blood Jim brought in and all it did was verify his suspicions. He knew that Jim had been in Washington DC researching Dr. Bizarro's work but no one had had a chance to ask him about what he found out yet. He was afraid to ask Jim about it in front of Ally just in case there was something Jim didn't want to say, so when Ally was redressing after her examination, Dr. Roberts called Jim out into the hallway to talk.

"Jim, I know you've been researching, find anything helpful?"

"I've got Joshua going over it a second time. I have a hard time believing what I found could be true."

"Want to talk about it?"

"Not really, but I know I should." Jim sighed, "Can we go into your office for a moment?"

"Sure." Dr. Roberts said as he led Jim down the hall. Once in his office, he pointed for Jim to take a seat then he shut the door and walked to his desk and sat down. Jim took a deep breath and then spoke what he knew.

"Bizarro was a very sick man. Apparently hired by Hitler during World War Two to create a superior soldier; a soldier with feline senses. Someone who could see in the dark, hear long range distances, someone who could be quiet as a mouse whilst infiltrating an enemies territory, agile enough to get through any sticky spot, someone who can do what other humans consider impossible for anyone besides a feline."

"I see."

"Well, I think that is why Bizarro's brother James hid the last journal, it would have been too embarrassing for his family to deal with if word ever got out."

"I see. So what is Joshua going to do?"

"I don't know. You see I didn't tell him about that part yet."

"What part, about Hitler?"

"No, I couldn't yet. To find out that his grandfather was hired by the worlds arch nemesis

Hitler and that he truly was a mad scientist, I think it would break his heart."

"Um, Jim…" The doctor interrupted. "There is something I think I should tell you since it seems you don't know yet."

Chapter 17

"She went to see another hypnotist?"

"Yes." The doctor acknowledged carefully. "Joshua realized how much more could be learned from another hypnotic episode so he talked her into it."

"I can't believe she did that again after what happened the last time!"

"It was actually a good thing I think. Joshua was able to find out more information about the history of the formula and we were able to determine that Ally is actually going through lives each time she transforms. We now know she is on life eight now so we need to be more careful from here on out." Just then Ally walked into the office and Jim jumped right onto her. "You went to see another hypnotist?"

"Yes." Ally spoke decisively and she continued explaining before Jim could ask any other questions or get any angrier. "And it really helped answer a few questions. It seems Joshua's Uncle James tried to kill me or actually kill Goldie when she was a cat in order to keep the formula from being found out."

"No, he didn't care about the formula he just didn't want Hitler to get his hands on it."

"Hitler?" Ally chimed up curiously.

"Hitler hired Bizarro to create the formula for a superior army so he could take over the world. If James hadn't kept it secret Hitler would have won World War 2 and succeeded in taking over the world!"

"Does Joshua know this?"

"Not yet." Jim admitted. Ally wanted to go home and call Joshua but the doctor spoke first.

"Before you two leave I must talk to you first." The doctor spoke up. They both sat down. "Thanks to the hypnosis the other day I can now confirm without a shadow of a doubt that Ally is definitely going through a felines a-typical nine lives and that Ally is currently on life eight right now."

"Life eight?" Jim said with shock now realizing how much he had missed while he was in DC. The doctor continued though knowing Jim would catch up.

"Each time Ally transforms into a cat completely, she comes out of it ever more weaker than before. Her DNA keeps changing and each time she turns human again, she faints for a moment as if her body can't handle the stress of changing. Jim you have to keep a close eye on her, she's only got one life left, so you've got to be careful."

"Doctor do you have a list of each change?" Jim asked.

"Yes." He said as he opened Ally's file. "There was the cliff she was pushed from, the Hollywood catastrophe, the CAT scan here in the hospital, the panic attack, the reporters in New York, the building fire, and then last nights hanging. That is seven used lives, she's on her eighth life now."

"Doctor," Ally spoke up. "I have a question, those were every time I turned completely into a cat, what about the times I almost did but stopped myself, like in the bathroom when I was scared about the future and began to change but Jim calmed me down or in the Hypnotists office when I started to transform but didn't go all of the way?"

"Ally you know I wish I had the answers but I don't. Those times did harm to your DNA strand but not as drastically as the times you changed all the way. I truly believe with the amount of DNA change you've gone through divided by the number of times you've changed and subtracted from the amount of DNA change you've got to go to get 100% feline DNA, you've got about one more major change to go."

"One more life you mean." Jim corrected.

"I think so. We've now come to that conclusion scientifically as well as spiritually."

"Then what?"

"Ally, I don't know. I wish I did! I wish I knew what to do to stop this but I don't!" Doctor Roberts cried nearly having an emotional break down "I don't know what to do! I almost called a vet!" He admitted horrifically.

When Jim and Ally got home they went directly upstairs. Jim had begun to understand Ally's determinacy to stay away from everyone in the house. Although they were just curious and concerned, they were too bombarding. They approached her immediately when she entered the house, they began asking their questions and although Jim wanted to tell them, he had no problem with them knowing, he just didn't feel like trying to explain something he was having such a hard time wrapping his head around. He apologized to them adding he would come down later and talk to them but that right now he just wanted to go upstairs with Ally and talk with her privately.

Once upstairs Jim closed the door behind him and went to the bed and sat down, Ally went to her dresser and took her hair down, then looked at her face in the mirror. Her golden brown hair framed her heart shaped face her deep green eyes staring back at her, she almost didn't recognize her face. She looked into the reflection of the room and saw Jim sitting on the bed, his head lowered and cupped in his hands as if he were tired or sad or both. She turned and went to him, she knelt down in front of him and took his hands into hers, her face was right in his and she smiled at him.

"It's going to be alright."

"I know it is." Jim half smiled wanting desperately to believe it but Ally could tell that his heart hadn't been in that sentence. She leaned forward and kissed him gently on the lips, when she pulled away slightly his eyes looked into hers. They were filled with confusion and love, sorrow and bliss. He had been so preoccupied from the night of prom, the entire month he spent in DC, then last night when he got home, he knew he had a job to do, to save Ally's life but he had been so swept up in his "work" he had all but forgotten the reason he had gotten into all of this in the first place. He was completely and unequivocally in love with Allison Catsworth.

All of the work and stress, all of the distractions, and grief could only for a moment make him forget, but one look, one kiss could bring him back tenfold to the love of his life. He knew without a doubt that no matter how long or how short their time was with each other it was worth it all just knowing her.

He leaned forward and kissed her again, pulling her into his arms, embracing her in a way that she hadn't felt for so long. She felt so safe and so loved; she felt all of her worries and stress all of the pain and agony in her life just melt away. She wasn't sure if it was the time away from each other, the knowledge that it could all be over at any time or the sheer fact that the both of them needed to feel something other than sadness but she gave herself wholly to Jim and he gave himself wholly to her. They shared an afternoon together that meant everything; it was an expression of their love that they had never experienced. Through all of the times they had the chance they never needed it as much as they needed to know and feel love today.

It was early evening when Jim finally made his way downstairs. The household was quiet, the phones weren't ringing, the TV and radio were not on, most of the lights had been turned off and Jim wondered for a moment if Bob had given everyone the night off. As Jim walked into the kitchen to find something to eat he noticed Bob sitting in a chair at the breakfast table his back to the door. He was just sitting there, staring off into the darkness and Jim wondered briefly if all of the stress had finally gotten to the old man. He wondered if he should disturb him by turning on the light but he decided he didn't need to. He walked into the kitchen and opened the refrigerator and stuck his face in looking for food. Bob finally spoke after a moment of this silence and what he said made Jim freeze.

"She is all I have left."

Jim didn't move a muscle, he wanted to stand up straight, to close the refrigerator door, to turn to face Bob, to offer some kind of support or at least say something comforting but he had nothing to offer. He closed his eyes, trying to think of something other than himself but he couldn't. Ally was everything to Jim the sheer idea of loosing her made his heart shatter in his chest and he was having a hard enough time dealing with that, but he hadn't once thought about what all of this was doing to her father. Finally Bob spoke again.

"After Ally's mother died I gave up. I raised my hands to the sky and I prayed for death because I knew that I didn't want to live in this world without her. And it wasn't until that night; the night that I nearly lost Ally that I realized I was still living in this world and I still had a very good reason to be here."

Jim heard Bob's words and understood them completely. "Mr. Catsworth I know you are upset and tired, we all are but…"

"Jim, promise me you will take care of her."

"Bob?" Jim asked cautiously, a sick, frightening feeling sunk in Jim's gut, as he comprehended Bob's words and tone of voice.

"Promise me that you will always look after her. Promise me that you will figure this thing out and save her..."

Ally had woken upstairs to find the room dark and empty. The sun had set and she was alone. She called out for Jim but he wasn't there and as she sat up in bed a feeling of panic swept over her. The human Ally would have simply realized that Jim went downstairs, but there was something in the air, an emotion permeated the air, something that her feline senses detected and it frightened her. Not the fact that the senses detected something or that she even had feline senses, that the emotions she felt were filled with so much sadness and doom. She quickly leapt from bed and grabbed her robe.

Jim was feeling uncomfortably nervous with the conversation at hand. Bob was eerily disturbing as he was speaking and Jim felt something bad was about to happen. As he walked over to the side light switch he flipped on the lights and took a good long look at Bob for the first time that night. Suddenly Jim's heart sunk to the pit of his stomach and he knew this was a situation he was definitely not prepared to be dealing with tonight.

"Bob, now listen to me, everything is going to be just fine you hear me?"

As Ally rushed down the stairs the commotion of her feet racing across the floor attracted George's attention and he emerged from the study just as Ally ran past him. He quickly followed feeling that there was something wrong and when he did, Rachel did too.

Jim had walked up carefully to the opposite edge of the table as Bob and was carefully trying to calm the situation down but Bob was too far-gone. He raised the little handgun in his right hand and aimed it against his head. A tear streaked down his face as he spoke.

"Promise me you will take care of her."

By now Jim knew a careful plea was not the solution to this particular problem and he knew that he needed serious help. He yelled now at Bob, yelled as loud as he could to try to get through to Bob as well as hopefully acquire somebody's attention, hopefully George's.

"Bob don't do it! How do you think Ally will deal with this?"

Just then Ally ran into the room, skidding to a stop when she saw the gun. George bumping into her as he too slid into the room, but before they could comprehend what was happening, Jim saw Bob's finger pulling the trigger. He leapt across the table, sliding hands first into Bob. He grabbed the gun and knocked the old man's chair over sending the both of them crashing to the floor. The shot resounded though and the bullet went through the wall but it wasn't the end. Bob refused to let go of the gun. The sound of the shot woke the rest of the household and George quickly grabbed Ally and shielded her from another possible shot but all she could do was watch in horror as Jim struggled on top of her father trying to pry an already smoking gun from his hands.

"Daddy!" Ally yelled but he wasn't listening to reason although reason was all Jim was trying to beat into the man.

"What the hell are you thinking? You could have shot Ally!" Jim yelled angrily.

"Just let me die! Maybe if I die God will let Ally live!"

"Daddy please!" Ally cried struggling with her own emotions as George held her back away from harms way.

"Look at what you are doing to your daughter!" Jim grabbed the father's face and pressed it down and left pointing his direction at Ally. "Look at her! Do you really want her to see you like this!" Jim yelled as he continued to try to beat the gun from Bob's hands. Bob slowly looked over at his daughter. She was crying and trying desperately to get away from George so she could go to her father, but George refused to let her anywhere near the gun. Ally was screaming and crying.

"Daddy! Daddy please!" She knew Jim was in danger of getting shot as well but she just couldn't help herself.

As Bob loosened his grip on the gun, Jim sent a powerful punch at Bob's face, knocking him out. As the man's head hit the floor, Jim retrieved the gun and threw it to the side of the kitchen then he looked up to see Ally crying, her face hidden in George's chest, his arms still around her but now as if in comfort, he had shielded her with his body but his eyes never left the scene, not until he knew the situation had been handled. As Jim stood up he didn't know what to do first, his heart was still pounding in his chest from the rush of adrenaline; the surge to not only want to save his father-in-law but his own life while he was at it. He hated what he had to do tonight but he was proud of himself and his quick reaction. So when he went to Ally to comfort her, to take over for George, he was hurt when she pushed him away and ran off.

Once Rachel saw the gun and the struggle she ran to the other side of the living room for safety. When Ally ran past her, tears streaming down her face Rachel began to worry. Rachel entered the kitchen she saw George standing there at the doorway. She saw Bob, comatose on the floor then she heard a loud slam as Jim punched the counter top.

"Damn it George! Why did you let her watch that!"

"I can only shield her from danger I can not shield her from life." And with that Jim turned on a heel and stormed out the backdoor, slamming it on his way out.

George was slightly worried about Jim but the sound of a second door slamming grasped his attention instead. He knew immediately it wasn't an echo and that in his own confusion, Ally had pushed away from not only Jim but him too. Rachel even turned to see that Ally's coat was gone.

"She ran out."

"Inform the household! Get Sam to watch Bob. Then find Jim and tell him."

Then George ran out the front door in search of Ally himself. As he ran across the street in the straightest shot he could think of he thanked the moon silently for shining so much of its white light down upon the land tonight for his eyes caught sight of Ally almost immediately and he was able to follow her up the hill and into the field.

"Jim." Rachel yelled into the darkness as she saw his silhouette leaning against the railing of the porch. "It's Ally. She's gone."

"What?" Jim exclaimed as he spun around to face Rachel.

"She ran out the front door, George is already trying to find her."

"Thanks." Jim exclaimed as he ran past Rachel into the house, through the kitchen and out the front door leaving it open wide. Rachel watched as she saw the three figures disappear into the darkness, and she prayed all would end safely.

Joshua had waited patiently in his room, curiously wondering what his aunt was looking into when she walked into his room holding something in her hands.

"It took me a while to remember where I hid it but…" She paused as she began to hand it over to Joshua. "I think this is what you are looking for." Joshua raised his hand to retrieve it ever so slowly so hopeful this was the what he had been looking for but afraid to get his hopes up. "I hope it will help her."

"Thank you Aunt Sophia." Joshua stated as he looked at the dusty journal in his hands.

"You are quite an amazing young man." Sophia proclaimed. Joshua stood to give her a hug, then she left his room. As he sat the journal down on his desk and turned on his light he flipped the cover open and saw crayon drawings. Confused at first, he flipped through the pages.

As Ally ran she never once looked back to see George and Jim both following her, they were just trying to catch up to her without enough breath to call out to her. All she knew was her emotions were up way too high, she needed desperately to get away from it all and she was scared. Scared of what she had seen, scared of turning into a cat, scared of losing her father. She ran into the woods, bare feet already bleeding from the rough terrain, legs too frozen from the cold air blasting on them to feel. She felt initially that for whatever reason running into the woods would help her calm, maybe that was the feline part of her. The human part of her however realized that the woods only scared her more. The darkness and shadows swarmed around her, sounds of the forest echoed through her ears and suddenly her senses seemed to intensify. She sensed more than a human ever should. Her eyes saw through the darkness illuminating the pathway, her legs seemed to strengthen, taking her further faster, her ears caught sounds of every critter here as well as the hefty footsteps of something speeding towards her.

As Jim caught up to George he gasped with air trying to speak.

"What happened?" George too nearly out of breath gasped with his explanation.

"She's too scared to stop." Jim knew he had to do something and although he was sure Ally was too far away already he had to call out after her. He had to attempt to get her to stop, especially in her current state. There were numerous dangers out here in the forest none the which had anything to do with reporters and psychos but all that had to do with nature's obstacles and animal predators.

"Ally!" He huffed as he recollected his breath, and tried again. "Ally stop!"

Tree branches slapped against Jim and George as they ran through the forest but they knew they couldn't stop. However every crack of a tree branch only sped Ally further away. She just couldn't stop. Her senses were unbearably heightened and although it was extremely frightening it was also extremely exhilarating – almost enlightening.

As she ran she saw everything, she saw everything with such clarity that she just couldn't immobilize herself. It seemed as if the human inside was gone and the cat had taken over. A wild sense of freedom and sovereignty had taken her over and it was all she could do to keep from changing one hundred percent and running off into the night forever.

However Jim knew these woods like the back of his hand. Growing up in this town, spending every day of his childhood out here exploring he knew that even in the darkness there were more dangers than imaginable, one of which was coming up way too quickly for his taste and he warned George of it.

"Cliff."

"When?"

"Soon."

As Ally approached it, seeing it clearly with the moonlight revealing the path ahead of her, the cliff wall across the ravine easily over one hundred feet tall she began feeling more and more frightened although she still couldn't stop. It was as if the feline inside was trying to get out and it was all she could do to stay human. But as the ravine came closer and closer Ally felt herself willing to let the feline come out if only to save her life. As she changed, her robe seemed to just float in the spot her body was last seen and Jim grabbed it as he flew past. Now he was following the feline and he wasn't going to stop until she was in his arms, not even if it meant going over the cliff with her. He refused to give up on her. As she leapt in the air to jump across the ravine Jim grabbed her. The sudden stop mid air was enough to nearly make her pass out due to lack of oxygen. And as Jims feet slid to the edge of the cliff and almost over, George showed up, grabbed the robe still hanging from Jim's free hand and yanked it backwards just enough to pull Jim and Ally away from the cliffs edge. As the both of them fell backwards to the ground in a pile of aching muscles and aching hearts George fell to his knees. He had come so close to going over the edge and the thing that really got to him was he didn't know why.

He sat there in wonder as he watched Ally change back and Jim cover her with her robe. Jim didn't speak, he was too tired, trying to catch his breath but Ally did. She apologized for running, she explained how she couldn't stop, how the feline senses took over, that she had lost all control and it felt so wild, so feral. After a few minutes of rest Jim helped her to her feet, they were sore and in pain but they worked. The three of them walked back home together.

Chapter 18

That night Joshua made a phone call to Ally's home and he informed Rachel that his Aunt Sophia and him were driving down. Joshua was so eager to see Ally, so excited to finally have in his possession the formula he couldn't sit still.

Jim was on the phone with Doctor Roberts when Joshua and Sophia walked in. Jim had told the doctor all about last nights happenings including the part where Ally went feline and hearing that Joshua became worried. He knew she was on life eight before and now she was on nine. The doctor thanked Jim for sending Karen Shafer down with the new blood sample and said he'd get on it right away then Jim hung up the phone and saw Joshua sitting there. He was overjoyed.

"Joshua! When did you get here?"

"Just now. How is Ally?"

"Fine for now. How are you doing?"

"I actually have news but would like to tell Ally first if you don't mind."

"Tell me what?" Ally asked as she walked down the staircase, she looked upon Joshua and smiled. "Back so soon?"

Ally offered Joshua something to drink as Jim took his aunt to the guestroom to drop off their bags. Bob and George were in the other room discussing security measures and Karen and Rachel talked in the kitchen. Joshua sat his bag down on the couch and pulled out the journal for Ally to see. "I found the cure!"

"You did?" Ally spoke with shock then plopped down on the couch.

"It is a rather complex formula but I'm sure Doctor Roberts will be able to figure it out. According to Bizarro's notes all we have to do is mix the chemicals together and inject you with it and it will change you back from a cat."

"But Joshua, I'm not a cat."

"So we'll have to change you."

"No way, Joshua" Ally sighed. "The next time I change is it. Life nine. And I don't know if that ends or not. I can't take any chances."

"I know it'll work."

"Yeah but Joshua," Ally began carefully, "I'm *transforming* into a cat. I'm not a permanent cat. I don't think that formula will work on me, it was meant to work on Goldie." She admitted having serious reservations on whether this would work.

"It has to work. It's what we've been looking for all of this time. It's why Jim and I did all of that research."

"I know Joshua but I'm not sure I want to test it on myself without knowing what it will do first."

"Then we'll test it on a cat."

"The idea of the formula is to change a cat back to its original human form, a regular cat won't have an original human form. Its original form would be the cat."

"Then we'll recreate the serum and change a human into a cat and then back again."

"I know you mean well Joshua but who would willingly risk their life for that kind of test?"

"I would." Joshua nearly cried. Ally smiled.

"I know you would, but I can't let you do that. Besides, I'm a different kind of test subject. I was reincarnated with the serum in me. That is completely different and almost impossible to recreate scientifically. I'm sorry Josh but I don't believe the serum will work on me."

"You're wrong!" Joshua cried as he ran out of the room.

"Joshua wait!" Ally called out immediately feeling bad about this. She began to chase after him. Joshua was so upset, he ran straight to the front door and right through it. Joshua was upset and crying, not paying attention to where he was going and Ally worried he was going to get himself hurt. "Joshua I'm sorry!"

Joshua finally stopped running when he heard her apologize. He caught his breath and turned to face Ally who was slowly coming to a stop. She bent over, placing her hands on her knees catching her breath and Joshua started walking back towards her when she heard something. At that very moment she heard screeching of tires as a car sped around the corner at high speed. It was heading directly towards Josh who was currently standing in the middle of the road.

"Joshua!" Ally yelled as she reacted. She ran to him. Pushed him out of the way with all of her might as the car ran right into her, throwing her body over the hood and roof of the car. The driver of the car slammed on the brakes and the car skid to a stop about thirty feet away. From the safety of the ground on the other side of the street, Joshua watched in horror as Ally's body twirled upwards, into the air, transforming into a cat and then landed with a thud on the ground. Joshua stood there watching, waiting to see if she stirred, waiting to see if she transformed back into a human and after a few moments of no movement he began to panic.

Joshua couldn't help but notice, wonder and worry why she hadn't changed back to human again. The cat was unconscious, not moving. Ally had been worried about her ninth life, not quite knowing what would happen when she used it, afraid, terrified to find out. And as Joshua stood there in shock and disbelief he realized, Ally had used up her last life, saving his life. He ran to the still cat and quickly checked for any vital signs, anything that would tell him that she was still alive and as he noticed a slight rising and falling of her chest cavity he realized, she was still alive.

"She's breathing." He spoke quietly to calm himself. Joshua, however, could tell Ally wasn't in very good shape. He had never had a pet before, and of course Ally wasn't a pet but being that she was now a cat and not changing back he feared that this was the end of the Ally that he knew. Everyone kept speculating that once the ninth life was used up Ally would die. It made sense but others would say; it won't happen, it can't. It's like when you're waiting for something big to happen and it seems like it's taking so long to get here that your mind suddenly starts thinking it'll never happen, so when it does happen, when the inevitable happens, you're not prepared.

Joshua looked up from the felines body to the driver of the car as he got out of his car and just stood there staring. He didn't know what to do. He wasn't sure if he should call for an ambulance or a vet. A few neighbors came out to gawk but no one said a thing.

Joshua looked back down at the cat, his friend Ally and began to cry. He was still a child but he had acquired such a strong bond with her and her family that the sheer idea of loosing her tore at his soul. But suddenly he realized that whatever happened Ally needed to be around her family and loved ones and for a brief moment Joshua was grateful that Ally had stayed the cat, because he scooped the lifeless body up into his arms and carried her. As he walked back towards the house, still no one reacted. They all watched on, horrified and distraught. No one moved and no one spoke.

No one in the house had even known they left he house. He could hear regular sounding conversations from various places throughout the house and Joshua's heart crumpled. This was his fault. He filled with such remorse. He was responsible for this and as he looked down at the small limp feline in his arms, hardly holding onto life, he began to cry.

The heart-felt wailing filled the house like a freight train. Everyone stopped speaking and ran to the living room to see what was going on. As their eyes took in the sight of this young boy, Joshua, holding a very dead looking orange cat struck them, the house filled with silence. Everyone's hearts literally sank to the pit of their stomach. Rachel began to cry already giving up. Bob fell to his knees. But Jim ran to Joshua determined to believe that she was not dead.

"Joshua what happened?"

Joshua looked at Jim with tears in his eyes, he had been trying to figure out what to say but he didn't know how to phrase it. He stuttered slowly through his staggered breathing just enough to say "She's still alive."

Suddenly the mood of the house perked up, there was still hope. Everyone scrambled to the unsaid plan B and Jim took the feline upstairs and placed the limp body on the bed. Bob called Doctor Roberts and Sandra called the vet. Joshua's aunt went to give him a hug but he couldn't be consoled, he was feeling too guilty for that. He went upstairs to tell Jim what happened. As he walked through the door of their bedroom Jim could sense he was mortified. No matter what happened, he knew he couldn't blame Joshua. This young boy had done more for them....

"It's all my fault! If she dies, it'll be my fault!" Jim got to his feet and went over to Josh. He took Josh's hands into his and spoke directly to him, his eyes into Josh's eyes.

"This is not your fault! You hear me? You didn't perform the scientific act that changed Goldie Givens. You didn't push Ally from the cliff, or try to hang her or any of the other things that took a life. You've done nothing but be her friend and do everything in your power to help her."

"But I did take a life! She saved me from being hit by a car! She used up her last life to save mine!" Joshua began crying harder. Jim didn't know what to say or to do, but he knew Joshua didn't need to continue to think he was responsible for this.

"You listen to me Joshua, Ally loved you. She would have tried to stop a speeding train if it meant saving your life, she would have done it for anybody. That's who she was. It was nothing you did or didn't do that put her in this predicament so I want you to stop thinking that it was. You are one of Ally's best friends and I know she would never blame you for this and so you shouldn't either."

"Really?" Joshua sniffed, trying to stop crying.

"Really.

Just then Bob ran into the room with the blood taking kit and began taking some of Ally's blood. Jim was curious about this action because he didn't know what it would help. Besides, there was so much going on he couldn't handle too much more.

"Bob, what are you doing?"

"Doctor Roberts made an excellent point just now over the phone. We've never had a chance to take any of the cats blood. As a full out one hundred percent cat the DNA will be absolutely feline, if she changes back to human, God willing, we'll be able to see by the strands how much longer she has."

"Is Doctor Roberts on his way?"

"He is. He'll be here in about twenty minutes." Just then Rachel ran into the room with another man.

"Jim this is Dr. Bing, he's a veterinarian."

"You brought a vet to look after my wife?" Jim shouted angrily.

"She is a cat, what better doctor is there?"

"She is first and foremost a human!"

"She is unconscious! A car has hit her and she is dying! A regular doctor isn't going to know anything about feline anatomy but a veterinarian does! For God's sake Jim! Let him help her!"

"Fine! I don't want to fight! Just do it! Do whatever it takes!" Jim screamed as he stepped aside to let the doctor in. His emotions had been so strained over this situation he couldn't tell what he was feeling anymore. All he knew was he didn't want Ally to die and he was at the point of trying just about anything.

Chapter 19

The veterinarian Dr. Bing was busily checking over Ally as Jim took a seat. His strength was almost completely depleted. He didn't know how much more stress he could take. He was just about to stand up and object to all of this and give up when Dr. Bing gave Ally a shot that within moments, slowly transformed her back into a human. Jim saw this happen along with everyone else in the room and everyone's mouth dropped open. Hundreds of questions were shooting through everyone's head when Jim spoke the most important question of all.

"How did you do that?"

Dr. Bing put the used syringe in a case and back into his medical bag then removed the clear plastic gloves he had been wearing and balled them up into his hand, then he looked up at Jim and spoke calmly.

"She was in pain. Stress, anxiety and fear seems to summon up the feline. I figured being in pain was keeping her feline."

"You know about her?" Bob asked knowing that the average tabloid follower wouldn't know quite enough to understand Ally's predicament that clearly.

"Rachel has kept me up to speed on the situation, she felt that my services may be needed at some point."

Jim looked over at Rachel standing next to him and thanked her. Just then Dr. Roberts walked into the room and saw Ally lying there human.

"She changed back?" He asked immediately expecting to see the cat lying there. Dr. Bing explained the situation the best he knew. Then they were interrupted by Joshua's sad voice speaking up from next to Ally on the opposite side of the bed.

"Doctors, shouldn't she be waking up now?"

Meanwhile, on the other side of the country in Hollywood, Joyce's home phone just rang. "This is the general manager for the Late Show with Johnny Carson. We are interested in having you on our show tonight."

"Really?" Cindy exclaimed with pure pleasure.

"Can we pencil you in for sometime this week?"

"Of course! When do you need me?"

"What does your schedule look like for tomorrow night?"

"Tomorrow night is clear." Joyce said as she wrote it down on a notepad next to her bed.

"Good, we'll need you in make up and wardrobe by 9:30, our people will call your people."

"Thank you!"

As Cindy hung up the phone she was so excited the first person she could think to share this with was Ally. She quickly dialed the phone number and waited with bated breath to hear her best friends' voice.

"Hello?" Jim asked with little emotion as he answered the phone.

"Jim? Its Cindy how are you?" She asked gleefully.

"Not well."

"Why? What's wrong?" She asked with worry immediately forgetting about her news.

"It's Ally."

"Is she okay?"

"She's… she's in a coma."

"Oh my God! What happened?" Cindy exclaimed with shock.

"She was hit by a car."

"Oh no…." Cindy gasped. She sat there for a moment, nothing but silence on the phone when she realized something. "What life was it?"

"Nine."

Cindy nearly dropped the phone. She was in shock, she didn't know what to do and she knew this was really bad news. "What can I do?" She asked knowing she had to be strong for her friend.

"I don't know. Look Cindy, I know you mean well, but I just don't feel like talking right now." Jim said sounding truly wiped out.

"I understand. Jim, listen, if there is anything you need, don't hesitate to call." Cindy offered hoping if there was something he needed, he would ask.

"I know."

"I mean it."

As Cindy heard Jim hang up the phone she sat there in despair. She had been so excited a moment ago, she was going on the late show and now, it didn't seem all that important. A dream of hers for years had finally come true and all that seemed important right now was Ally. She sat there on her bed trying to figure out what she could do for the longest time when she came up with an idea. She would go on the late show. She would make her appearance in front of an audience of thousands and she would say what needed to be said.

She then decided to make one more phone call.

"How's she doing?" Sandra asked as she walked into the bedroom the next morning. Ally hadn't moved, Doctor Roberts had set her up on a breathing machine, heart sensors and all sorts of machines to keep track of her. He even set up a brain wave machine to keep track of any REM sleep she may be experiencing. He didn't know what to expect or what could happen next so he wanted to be prepared by having all of his resources at his fingertips.

Jim looked up at Bob as he walked into the room. He too had large black circles under his eyes as he hadn't slept all night. By the looks of things no one had slept and the moods were very low. No one knew what to do if Ally didn't wake up soon. According to the doctors the longer she remained in this coma the worse it could potentially be.

"It's time for the Late Show with Johnny Carson, and here's your host..." Came the beaming strong voice of the announcer.

Cindy sat in her dressing room listening to the spokesperson make the regular greetings and she listened to the crowd cheer. She knew what she had to do tonight, but she was still frightened and worried. She prayed the world would understand what she needed to do and accept her for it but it still didn't help relax all of the enormous butterflies in her stomach.

Joyce had been flipping through channels tonight, restless yet wide-awake. She had been feeling bad that she hadn't had any time for Ally for so long. After breaking all of this to Jim and then Ally, she and Brad just felt it best to lay low. Then, after seeing all of the chaos those videos and pictures caused she truly felt sorry for doing it. She wished there was a way to change things or to help make them better but she didn't know what she could do. She was just a small time reporter.

As she continued to flip through the channels she wasn't paying attention to much as her mind wondered to the good old times. The day she met Ally in the lunchroom line. How they laughed so hard that day and knew almost immediately that they would be life long friends. Then there was the day Ally introduced Cindy to Joyce. The three of them became almost inseparable, they did everything together, shopped, studied and hung out, they were as close as sisters and now everything had changed. Joyce and Ally weren't talking, no one had heard from Cindy since she became a big star…

"Please help me in welcoming our first guest Miss Cindy Recio!"

Joyce changed the channel before comprehending the name, but once she did she changed the channel back. As she watched her old friend walk on to the stage of the late show she suddenly felt very good. Her heart jumped for the excitement she felt for her friend. She began jumping on her bed screaming.

"Oh my God! She made it! Cindy's on the Johnny Carson show!" Brad woke from the pillow next to her and squinted at the TV.

Doctor Roberts and Doctor Bing were sitting in the dining room downstairs going over their notes, sharing ideas, simply trying to figure things out when they heard the maid in the other room turn up the volume to the TV. They looked at each other, decided without words that it was time for a break and walked into the darkened living room. They both stopped at the doorway and listened to the conversation already in progress.

"I know you want to discuss my new movie but I have something more important to me that I want to discuss." Cindy began already interrupting the hosts beginning remarks. "I know that most of the world knows the story of "Ally Cat" heck, I've even heard a few of the jokes you've said about her on your previous shows, but I want to set the record straight tonight. Ally Cat's full name is Allison Catsworth and she is my best friend!"

Everyone in the audience began murmuring amongst themselves but Cindy ignored their shock and continued. "You may remember the video of Ally while she was in Hollywood, she was with me. I know my publicists decided it would be best to pretend it didn't happen, but it did! Ally is my best friend and almost everything you've read about her life is only a fraction of it. She is a great person…"

Doctor Roberts excused himself and briskly walked up the stairs to the bedroom where Jim had been sleeping in a chair next to Ally's bedside. He shook Jim awake and told him he needed to come down stairs and hear this. Jim stammered out of the chair, grabbed his robe and followed the doctor downstairs. When they walked into the living room Jim stopped when he saw Cindy's face on TV. He almost didn't know what to think. He listened to her words for just a few seconds when he understood so much.

"Ally is a hero! You all have seen the past videos but have you all seen this one?" She asked as she cued the cameraman to flip on the videotape she had given him before the show began.

Everyone watched as a video recorder had captured a young boy swinging on a front yard tire swing. The boy was smiling and laughing and he spoke "Watch this, daddy!" But then something emerged from the bottom right corner of the screen. The father behind the camera recognized something taking place and so he moved his camera to record the action. He watched a boy run past him and heard a woman's voice yelling out "Joshua stop!" He then watched as the young boy Joshua stopped running and turned to look at the woman who then came into view of the camera. It was Ally.

She looked tired and she bent over to catch her breath but right then a loud screech from behind the cameraman startled him and he quickly turned with the camera to record a car speeding around the corner. Then he followed that car right back to where the boy was standing. Ally screamed for Joshua then ran to him as fast as she could and pushed him out of the way of the speeding car, saving his life. But she couldn't get out of the way in time and was hit by the car instead.

The cameraman kept rolling as her body flipped over the cars hood and he stayed focused on her as she turned feline and plopped down onto the dusty road. The video stayed focused on the unmoving cat for the longest time when Cindy gave the motion to pause the tape. Then the TV cameras returned back to Cindy who immediately began talking.

"Ally saved that boys life by sacrificing hers!" The audience gasped but Cindy continued. "But she is not dead. Not yet anyway. She is in a coma." Cindy paused trying to keep from getting emotional; she needed to keep track of what she was doing here tonight. "Anyone who has been keeping track of this ongoing tabloid-made-sitcom knows that Ally used up her ninth life in that moment and no one knows what's going to happen to her now. Well I happen to know differently! Her doctors have found something that might actually cure her!" The audience began murmuring again, but Cindy spoke over them. "Yes they have, but they can't try it unless she wakes up. Now I'm telling you all this because I know that Ally has touched your lives. Anyone who has spent even a minute with her, knows what kind of wonderful person Ally is. So I know that I'm not asking for a lot tonight when I ask you all for this: Most doctors believe that the sound of music, friends' voices, compassionate expression, even prayers, can be heard by coma patients. It is a known fact that coma patients can hear those loved ones talking to them. It can help wake them out of a coma!

Allison Catsworth is in a coma. So maybe, if everyone yells out how much they love her and want her to come back, maybe she'll hear our words and prayers and wake up! So those of you who care, those of you who want to see this story end happily, I'm asking you as a fellow friend to repeat these words with me, Save Allison Catsworth!"

Cindy paused for a moment to see if anyone would say it, the crowd was silent. At first Cindy felt maybe she had overstepped her boundaries, maybe she had been mistaken in thinking that the American people would feel the same way as her. But Cindy truly believed that maybe they just needed coercion so she said it again, "Save Allison Catsworth!"

She waited another moment; one person began to say it, but grew too shy to continue. Cindy knew if this were going to work she'd have to be their leader. She said it again.

"Save Allison Catsworth!" A few people joined her. She began to chant it. "Save Allison Catsworth!"

The rest of the audience began chanting it. Even the host of the show started chanting it, "Save Allison Catsworth!" And suddenly everyone began chanting, "Save Allison Catsworth."

Joyce had been watching and through her tears she was chanting it as well "Save Allison Catsworth!" She ran to her bedroom window and threw it open and she yelled out to the sleeping neighborhood, "Save Allison Catsworth!"

Ally's entire household was crying. Everyone looked up to Jim who was still standing at the doorway, smiling through his tears. When a news reporter broke into the late show and began speaking.

"We apologize for interrupting the show but we are now taking you to Times Square, where something remarkable is happening…"

"We are here reporting from Times Square where a large group of people had been watching the late show and felt emotionally inclined to begin chanting, sir can you tell our viewers what is happening here?"

The reporter tipped the microphone to the man and the uproar of people chanting the words save Allison Catsworth flooded the speakers. The man spoke loudly into the microphone.

"It's about saving her! It's about saving Allison Catsworth!" Then the man turned to a group of people who had been standing behind him and raised his fist to help lead the chant, "Save Allison Catsworth! Save Allison Catsworth!"

"This just in," another reporter said as the TV cameras clicked over to her. "It's amazing, simply amazing! We are getting reports from around the country that people have emerged from their homes in the middle of the night and they are all joining in the chant to save this woman; Allison Catsworth."

Jim ran upstairs and turned on the radio to a station that was reporting much of the same and then turned it up so Ally could hear. How he prayed Cindy was right, that maybe this kind of encouragement would help bring Ally out of this coma.

Bob and George carried the TV upstairs and set it up. “Listen to that Ally!” The world was chanting “Save Allison Catsworth!”

Jim stood by Ally’s side. He took her hand into his and spoke into her ear. “Ally if you can hear me, listen to this. Listen to all of these people. They’re speaking to you. They all want you to wake up just as much as I do. Can you hear them baby? Do you hear them?”

As Ally opened her eyes she saw whiteness. The brightest, whitest light she had ever seen. And she felt herself being drawn toward it. As she seemed to just float through it she realized she was floating through the clouds, soft, white fluffy clouds, tickled her senses as she noticed herself being drawn closer and closer to a figure standing before her. As the dark silhouette of the figure stood before her, waiting for her arrival she wondered silently, could this be God?

Chapter 20

Doctor Roberts, Bob, Sandra and the rest of the household went up stairs to see if this was having any effect on the coma patient. They all watched and waited with bated breath, hoping, praying for Ally to wake, hoping that this would work. Jim kept one eye on Ally and one on the TV he couldn't believe how much love the world had for Ally but then again, he could.

Ally had floated all of the way to that silhouette in Heaven and now she stood before him, silently wondering who he was. Finally the figure stepped forward as if stepping into a spotlight and Ally was able to see his face. The face was old, wrinkled and aged, bright blue eyes seemed to reflect the blue sky surrounding him and the white hair and a white lab coat seemed to make him blend into the white cloudy surroundings but his voice boomed loudly as if he were a lot stronger than he looked.

"I am Doctor Auguste Bizarro."

"Dr. Bizarro? Really? I have so many question for you."

"All in good time my child."

“Where am I?”

“It is your minds vision of heaven.”

“Dr. Bizarro…”

“Please, call me Auguste.”

“Auguste.” Ally corrected. “Can you tell me what is going on?”

“I brought you here to help you.”

“Help me?”

“To help you understand.”

Jim sat back down next to Ally’s bed, he kept hoping that maybe this chanting would help wake her up but a long time had already passed and still nothing. The news media was still airing the countrywide chanting while showing video of Ally’s previous endeavors when he heard a commotion outside. Doctor Roberts went to the window and opened it to see most of the towns’ people, still in their sleep wear and robes, walking towards the house chanting. Some of them brought candles, while others went and began knocking on neighbors’ doors to have them come out and join them. Before long almost everyone in the town had gathered around outside the house for a midnight, candle light vigil to chant and pray all in hopes of saving Allison.

The television was still blaring with news reporters doing stories about Ally and her chanters. They showed footage of her many times of transformation and then kept going back to the news coverage spreading across the country of thousands of people chanting the chant "Save Allison Catsworth!"

"So do you understand now Ally?" Auguste asked once he was finished explaining the situation.

"I think I do, but how will I know that it worked?"

"Your scientists will have their ways." Just then a noise seemed to grow from below Ally's feet and it began growing louder.

"What is that?" Ally asked with pure curiosity.

"It is for you."

"For me?"

"It is everyone with whom you have touched a life. They are all chanting, praying for you to wake up."

"But I am in Heaven. I'm already dead?"

"No, you are just visiting and now I need to send you back home."

"But wait I have so many more questions…"

"All in good time. I have answered all that I can. Now you must go back with that knowledge and survive."

It was about two AM that the local news station drove up in their van and began recording the vigil, asking questions about it in hopes of getting a part of this story. Jim kept sitting next to Ally. He kept talking to her over the loudness of the TV and commotion outside. He kept telling her how much he loved her, how everyone wanted her to wake up. Many hours had passed since the chanting began and although everyone was still very excited about it, Joshua could tell that if Ally didn't wake up soon, the people would give up and go back home. He began to pray silently for a miracle, for Ally to wake up, for all of the peoples hopes and prayers and chants would be heard and that something good would come of this. He was completing his prayer when something did happen.

The heart monitor hooked to Ally had seemed to be chanting along with the crowd all night long. The beats seemed to stay right on cue with the people but all of a sudden Doctor Roberts realized something in the tune had changed. He went over to the heart monitor and turned up the volume so he could hear it better. Suddenly he realized, it chimed an extra beat. Jim turned to question the doctor but it did it again. It was as if Ally's heart was jumping for joy, waking to the promise of a new day. Doctor Roberts took out his stethoscope and began checking Ally's pulse. Her breathing became deeper and Jim could see that something was happening. He gripped a hold of Ally's hand tighter and spoke loudly to her.

"Come on baby, wake up! You can do it!"

The entire household had gathered in the room. Everyone was holding his or her breath waiting, wondering when Doctor Roberts finally looked up from his patient and spoke to them.

"I think she's coming out of it!"

Everyone wanted to cheer but they all still waited, they all wanted the proof, they all wanted to see her move. And suddenly she did. Her hand twitched and Jim nearly fell from his chair. He looked over at Ally, tears in his eyes and he too was holding his breath. Then another twitch, she was moving. Everyone gathered around the bed, all holding hands, all crying when slowly, Ally's eyelids flickered. Everyone gasped, waiting, wondering. Holding their breath expectantly, afraid to exhale, when Ally's eyes finally opened and she looked upon her family.

Cheers of rejoicing erupted from the household, everyone hugged one another and Joshua ran to the window and yelled down to the chanting people below,

"She's awake! Allison Catsworth is awake!"

The crowd erupted in cheer and applause. The news reporters caught that on tape and immediately aired it to the local station that broadcasted it on the spot, then moments later, the reporters on the station Jim had on in the bedroom began reporting the news. Ally watched it with tears in her eyes from her bed not quite understanding it all when Jim filled in her questions with answers.

"Cindy did this. Cindy began the chant last night and everyone just joined in. The entire world has been awake all night repeating the words Save Allison Catsworth over and over again."

Bob left the room to go downstairs and see about the reporters. When he opened the front door Cindy was approaching.

"Oh my God, it's you!"

"I just heard, she's awake?" Cindy asked as she walked in the door.

"Yes. How did you get here so quickly?" Bob asked in shock knowing well just four hours ago she had been in California on the late show.

"I'm a famous movie star now, the job came with perks like my own private jet." She smiled as she walked in the door. She ran upstairs as fast as she could after hearing the news on the taxicab's radio and burst in the bedroom door. Everyone in there turned to see her, making a clear path of view to Ally still laying there in the bed. Ally looked upon her friend and smiled and Cindy went to her and hugged her.

That morning Ally had Doctor Roberts perform all of the necessary tests and like she had said to him, like Auguste had told her that night, he was able to confirm that her DNA strands had reverted completely back to her original human DNA. The feline DNA was no longer in her system and had completely cleansed itself from her body. Once he was absolutely sure he asked Ally about it.

"You say Doctor Bizarro came to you in your dreams?"

"Either that or I was in heaven."

"And he told you that the cat was gone?"

"He did."

"Did he explain anything to you about it?"

"He said that when I was born as Goldie Givens I was born with a human soul but when Goldie died she was a cat. There is a difference between human and feline souls so when I was reincarnated as Ally I was given both souls, human and feline. The human soul was with me all of the time but the feline soul came out when I was in trouble. Auguste told me that once the feline soul had used up all of its nine lives it went on to heaven leaving me with one soul, my original human soul."

"So now you are one hundred percent human, you'll never change back into a cat again?"

"I don't think so."

"Oh."

"You sound disappointed doctor." Ally smiled.

"I'm not, I'm happy for you… it's just that, it's over. I am happy that it is over and that it ended well, I just am, well, I guess disappointed is the right word after all. I was hoping that there would be more of a scientific explanation for this, you know?"

"I understand, doctor."

A few hours later Joshua came into the room to see Ally. She saw him and smiled brightly, looking forward to talking to him when she realized he looked very sad and worried. She patted the side of her bed for him to sit beside her then asked him what was wrong.

"I nearly killed you. I ran into the street and nearly got hit by that car and if I wouldn't have been there you wouldn't have gotten hit saving me and none of this would have happened."

"But it all ended well."

"Yeah but we didn't know that. We didn't know what would happen once the ninth life was gone, you risked your life to save me."

"I guess I did." Ally smiled.

"But you shouldn't have."

"Why not?"

"Because I wasn't worth the risk."

"Joshua I want to tell you something and I don't quite know how to say it so I'll just say it."

"What is it Ally?" Joshua asked with concern.

"Joshua, you're my hero."

"What?"

"You are my hero. If it weren't for you I don't know what I would have done."

"Really?"

"Of course. You believed in me from the beginning. You did everything you could to help me. You helped Jim with the research, you knew I had to get hypnotized again and came down to help me with it. You found out some really difficult things about your family and dealt with it, you even stood up to your Uncle for me. If you hadn't been there to bring me home yesterday I don't know what would have happened to me. You truly are my hero."

"I did do all that, didn't I?" Joshua smiled brightly. Ally hugged him tightly. A few moments later Jim walked into the room.

"So it's a miracle."

"It seems so." Ally said as she finished her hug with Joshua and he left the room.

"The cat is gone?" Jim asked just to confirm.

"The cat is gone."

"And there aren't any residual side effects, no chance of it ever turning up again?"

"Not that I can foresee."

"Are you okay?"

"Honestly just a little bit sad, I think I'll miss it."

"What the popularity?"

"Well that yes, but the cat also."

"What do you mean?" Jim asked as he sat down next to Ally.

"I was just honing in on the feline abilities. I was learning how to see in the dark, to hear long range, to react with the agility of a feline…"

"And you won't have that anymore?"

"Probably not." Ally said. She could see that Jim didn't quite understand so she explained further. "It's like the cat was part of me and I spent all of my time fighting it instead of accepting it and learning more about it."

"Hind sight is twenty-twenty."

"I guess."

"So are you ready?" Jim asked standing back up again and offering Ally his hand.

"Yes." Ally smiled as she stood from the bed. As they walked downstairs everyone looked up at them and smiled happily. They all made a clear path to the front door for Ally and Jim. George even opened up the door for them. As the bright light of day shone in through the door it nearly blinded Ally for a moment but she kept walking out into the daylight. Once outside she heard the immediate eruption of cheering fill her ears as her eyes focused in on thousands of people, loved ones, friends, townspeople and strangers who had all gathered at the house to see how Ally was doing and give their congratulations and well-wishes.

As the day progressed Ally was able to reconnect with all of the people who had once been a part of her life, those who had their lives affected by Ally and those who just wanted to share their support. It was a good feeling for Ally to know that it was finally over and yet, it was all about to begin. From the night of that celebration at the waterfall her life had seemed to just stop, even though the world kept moving on. She had been stuck in this place where she couldn't move forward, but now she could. Now she knew there was nothing standing between her and Jim's marriage and their future.

Her father Bob had finally found love again with Rachel the assistant. Cindy's popularity had grown ten fold and Joyce had apologized and was back in Ally's life. It seemed life was great. Nothing could destroy her happiness, nothing could take it away.

Just then, Ally heard something and she turned to hear the faint sound past the people, past the trees, the homes, past the cars and down the road, she saw with perfect vision the small silhouette of a cat watching her. Her focus was caught on it for only a moment before Jim interrupted her concentration and brought her attention back to the people.

A moment later she glanced over that way again to see if the cat was still there. It was gone.

Ally wondered for only a moment if she had hallucinated, if she had even seen that cat. How could she have heard it at such a great distance over the roar of the crowd around her. How could she have seen the perfect shape of that cat so far away and know without a doubt that it was a cat she was looking at? As she smiled and spoke to yet another friend she wondered silently, was the cat in her really gone?

Chapter 21

"I'll be Ally!" Jenny called out to Johnny from the other side of the large oak tree in the front yard.

"I'm George, the bodyguard." Johnny declared as he went right into character and started the game. "Ally look out!" He yelled as he ran to her, yanking out his water gun and squirting a few shots towards an imaginary foe to his left.

When he was certain Ally was safe, he got up and looked at her, "It's not safe here, we need to move." He then took her by the hand and stealthily led her up the hill to the side of the house, portraying himself as quite the professional bodyguard.

Grandma watched them from the upstairs living room window and smiled at her sweet grandchildren. Life had been good to her. She had a wonderful husband. Many great friends. Her daughter had married a wonderful man and had given her two wonderful grandchildren. She couldn't ask for anything more.

That night as she tucked her grandchildren into bed, she kissed each on their forehead. "Grandma," Jenny called out sleepily. "Did Ally live happily ever after?"

"Yes she did sweetheart. Her life was wonderful."

"That really was a wonderful story." She cooed thinking dreamily of how happy it made her.

Johnny however was play-shooting the bad guys from behind his pillow. "I would have protected her. Those reporters wouldn't have stood a chance against me!"

Grandma smiled. "You're a good boy." She spoke as she placed the pillow flat on the bed and tucked him in again. "Time for bed kids, we have an early morning. Your parents will be here to pick you up."

"Awe!" They cried. "Can't we stay?" The children knew their summer visit was almost over. They had been looking forward to getting back home, to their friends and toys, but it was always so sad having to say goodbye. It was the worst part about visiting someone, the ending.

"I love you both very much." Grandma spoke sweetly as she looked back at the children laying in bed like angels. She flipped the light switch down, taking one last look and then closed the door to their bedroom.

The next morning the children really slept in. They hadn't heard Grandma tinkering in the kitchen. They hadn't smelled breakfast cooking. They didn't hear grandpa on his riding lawn-mower.

They slowly crawled out of bed, slipped their slippers on to their feet and sleepily shuffled down the hallway to the stairs. When they arrived at the top of the stairs they saw their parents sitting on the couch. Their father was holding their mother who was crying. Their grandfather had his head in his hands.

"What's wrong, mom?" Jenny called out as she and Johnny walked down the stairs.

Their mother looked up quickly and wiped the tears from her eyes. She smiled at them and held out her arms. They ran into her arms and hugged her and sat down on her lap. Their father kissed the top of Johnny's head as he pulled him into his arms. It was a wonderful reunion with a sadness in the air.

"Children something happened last night. Something very sad."

Two days later the family arrived at the church. Sadness had overtaken everyone. There was very little said. If tears were words they would have cried a novel, but no one could answer the question, why. There were sad smiles, which to Johnny and Jenny seemed to be a contradiction. How could you be crying and your heart be hurting and yet smiling with tears on your cheeks? Emotions were confusing and so was the situation, but their parents had explained it and they knew what had happened.

The funeral service was long and there were so many people. People that Johnny and Jenny had never met. They were hugged by so many strangers, and told wonderful stories about their grandmother. It made them happy to hear the stories but it wasn't the same as having her here with them.

They watched from their seats as their grandfather was greeted by so many people. An older woman, about Grandma's age, walked up to him and wrapped her arms around him. She said, "Ally was a wonderful friend." To which he acknowledged, "Thank you Cindy."

At the cemetery Johnny and Jenny held each others' hand. They stared at the headstone. They couldn't believe their eyes. They had always knew their grandmother by the name Grandma. Their grandfather had always called her honey or dear. Their mother had always called her mom. How could they not have known her name was Allison?

They stared at the headstone and then looked at each other, their eyes open wide. Their faces both spelled the question they were both thinking but were too afraid to ask. "Had the story been true?"

The pastor spoke about Allison's life, about her family, her legacy. He didn't say anything about the story she had shared with the kids but he hinted about something a long time ago.

Allison had taken her husband's last name, but her headstone spelled it out to the children very clearly.

Allison Catsworth-Brooks
"Ally Cat"

There was a cat's face engraved on the side of the stone. The kids knew she loved cats, had always had one. Had always fed the strays. They could see how the nickname could fit with her name but it didn't mean the story had been true.

They learned their grandfathers name is Jim. They met Joyce and Brad, they overheard a Sandra Pike talking to their mother. They met a really old man in a wheelchair who introduced himself as Mister Roberts. The characters were all here… all except…

"Jim, I am so sorry I'm late." A man slightly older then their parents declared as he walked in the door. He went right up to their grandfather and hugged him, embracing him for the longest time. They watched their grandfather weep in the man's arms but then looked up and smiled at the man. "Joshua, I knew you would come."

The grandchildren were both sitting on the couch watching the people, watching all of this happen. Untouched paper plates with cheese and crackers sat on their laps. If they could read each others' minds they knew they were thinking the same thing but then they'd shake it off. Couldn't be.

The afternoon turned to evening and most of the people who had gathered in their grandparents house had left, shy a few close friends. Their mother was in the kitchen with a few of the ladies and their grandfather was in his den with their father and the man who's name was Joshua. The grandchildren had fallen asleep on the couch a while ago apparently, and someone had covered them with blankets.

As they awoke, wiping the sleep from their eyes, they stared at each other again. What words could be spoken? The childhood fantasies of imaginary tales would not be strong enough to bring their grandmother back.

They sat on the couch, looking down at their shoes. Too sad to go play, to awake to go to bed. Their family had let them sleep and now the night had come and it hadn't brought anything different. Until…

Meow.

They looked at each other curiously then over towards the sound.

Meow.

They heard it again. It was small. Quiet. If they hadn't had been sitting there doing nothing they wouldn't have heard it. They looked back at each other, eyes open wide and they both came to the same exact conclusion at the same exact moment. They leapt to their feet and ran to the back door as fast as their little legs could take them. Then they slid to their knees directly in front of the sliding glass door and laid eyes on the miniature beige kitten sitting there before them.

It hadn't been frightened when they arrived. In fact it placed its small fuzzy paw on the glass as if it were reaching for them. Johnny slowly slid the door open as Jenny sat there quietly patting her lap. She watched in amazement as the tiny little kitten climbed up into her lap and curled into a ball. She looked up at Johnny who looked down at her and their mouths opened in awe. Then they both called out to the house at the top of their voices;

"She came back!"

Grandma's home!"

Their mother and two older ladies ran in from the kitchen, their father, grandfather and Joshua ran upstairs from the den. The light in the dining room flicked on blinding the kids for a moment as they looked at all of the adults standing around them, staring down at them, a small kitten sleepily laying in Jenny's arms. Jenny stood to show the family.

"Grandma came back."

Their mother started crying and Cindy held her, but Cindy was looking diligently at the children. Their grandfather stumbled into the wall and their father went to support him as Joshua stepped forward towards the children.

"May I see her?" He carefully asked as he held out his hands towards the kitten. Jenny carefully placed the small fuzzy ball into Joshua's hands. He stared at the tiny kitten for the longest moment before it slowly lifted its fuzzy head and open its eyes to look at him. Petite green eyes sleepily looked into his eyes. He looked deeply at the kitten, not wanting to think it possible yet not wanting to dismiss it either. He felt a warmth in this kittens eyes, a friendliness. Something about her encouraged him to do it, to say it. He spoke slowly, carefully, with a hesitant question in his quivering voice; "Ally?"

The kitten smiled at him, began purring and then laid its head back down. It curled into a tight little ball, its gold tail draped over his palm. As he looked up at the ladies, then back at his old friend Jim, he smiled shyly and raised his shoulders in a shrug.

No one said what the children had been thinking. No one needed to. The cute golden fuzz ball of a kitten had found a permanent loving home and it slept soundly with that knowledge.

www.KathleensBooks.com

About the Author:

Kathleen J. Shields is a very creative, highly imaginative and extremely dedicated, hard working individual. She runs her own website and graphics design company, Kathleen's-Graphics, and has published various books; from fully-illustrated rhyming stories for ages 4 and up, children's chapter books for ages 8 and up, and young adult stories with plans for a few romantic mysteries stories as well.

Kathleen has been writing poetry and stories for years; both for fun and for hire in custom greeting cards and for local speaking engagements. She enjoys sharing her stories and talking with children and adults about how they too can write if they put their mind to it.

She has also started a blog with inspirational and educational posts both regarding her endeavors as an author as well as a business woman and Christian. Her views are always light-hearted and thought-provoking and are intended to get the reader thinking.

Her fully-illustrated rhyming children's stories, the Hamilton Troll Adventures, are inspirational as well as educational. These stories are engaging and amusing and provide informative descriptions of various animal characteristics, vocabulary words and definitions, all while incorporating real-life situations that young children can face. Each story introduces at least one additional character, presents new obstacles to overcome, teaches something new, all while imparting a positive impression. This is a terrific series for bedtime stories and young readers, as well as readers who are young at heart.

For more information about the author, the various books she has written and plans to write, please visit: **www.KathleensBooks.com** or follow her blog at **www.KathleenJShields.com**

Made in the USA
Lexington, KY
27 October 2019